Suddenly all the anger of years burst into flame.

'I don't want your concern. Or your interest, Trent Livingstone. I don't want anything to do with you. *I* want to be left alone just as much as you do. So why don't you get the *hell* out of here and we'll agree to ignore each other for the rest of the summer? *Out!*'

His eyes narrowed. It was quite plain he was not intimidated by her rage; equally plain that her words had made an impact on him. With a strange note in his voice he said, 'OK—I'm leaving. But don't count on my not coming back. When and how it suits me.'

HAPPY ENDING

BY

SANDRA FIELD

MILLS & BOON LIMITED
ETON HOUSE   18-24 PARADISE ROAD
RICHMOND   SURREY   TW9 1SR

First published in Great Britain 1991
by Mills & Boon Limited

© Sandra Field 1991

Australian copyright 1991
Philippine copyright 1991
This edition 1991

ISBN 0 263 77124 5

Set in Times Roman 10 on 11½ pt.
01-9106-56937 C

Made and printed in Great Britain

CHAPTER ONE

THERE was a man in her bed.

Nicola blinked, and blinked again. He did not disappear.

He was indisputably real; although, to be accurate, he was on her bed, not in it. Lying flat on his back on top of the white chenille bedspread, his eyes closed. Snoring. And, she decided, wrinkling her nose in distaste, not only snoring but drunk, for a whisky bottle, two-thirds empty, rested in the curve of one arm and the air reeked of its fumes.

Perhaps she had made a mistake. Perhaps it wasn't her bed.

She took a long, steadying breath. She must have made a mistake, and entered the man's side of the cabin rather than her own. Olivia had specified the door on the left, but Olivia, even in the two short interviews Nicola had had with her—and despite the fact that she seemed to be running a successful writers colony—had not struck Nicola as a woman anchored in practicalities. That was it. The other door was the door to her side of the cabin. This one belonged to the unknown drunk.

Having no desire to wake him, for he was large enough to take up a considerable proportion of the three-quarter bed, Nicola quietly backed out of the room and crossed the living-room to the double doors that led outside, picking up her suitcase as she did so. The inner wooden door opened smoothly enough, but the hinges squealed on the old-fashioned screen door and nothing could have prevented the loud, aggressive snap with which it shut behind her. She scurried down the grey-painted steps and across the strip of grass, then climbed the steps to the other half of the cabin and pulled open the screen, stepping inside.

Wrong again, Nicola thought grimly. This side of the cabin was already occupied. A litter of books and papers surrounded the computer on the table, while various articles of male clothing of varying degrees of cleanliness were scattered over the furniture and the floor. An array of dirty glasses and plates adorned a smaller table by the hearth.

She would be willing to swear that the occupant of this room was the man with the whisky bottle.

Out she went and across to the other side, letting both screens bang as loudly as they liked. She dropped her case in the living-room—which, she now noticed, showed no signs of occupation at all and was indeed scrupulously clean and tidy—and marched back into the bedroom. The man had not changed position. He was still snoring.

Her lips compressed, Nicola surveyed him from head to toe. Or rather, from toe to head, for the first thing that caught her attention was that he was wearing leather workboots that had left dirt on her bedspread. *Her* bedspread. His jeans were soft and faded, fastened at his waist with a belt as worn as the boots. His shirt, partly hauled out of the belt, was also light blue denim, and was overdue for a wash; liberal amounts of the whisky appeared to have dribbled across one of the pockets. The top button was open, revealing a triangle of tanned skin. As her eyes moved up to his face her lashes flickered, and she took another of those deep, steadying breaths.

Drunk and snoring though he was—the snore had now changed timbre to a kind of low rumble in his chest— he was extremely good-looking. Although good-looking was too pallid a word, she thought, scowling to herself. His jaw might be slack in sleep, but it was a jaw to be reckoned with, squared off and indicative of a strong will. His nose had an intriguing bump in it which bespoke character; from his nostrils a well-indented groove ran to his upper lip, which had been sculpted in a long curve that fascinated her. She dragged her eyes away. His hair was blond. Another inadequate word, she decided irritably. But how else could you describe the streaked, thick mane that decorated her pillow?

She was wasting time. What she had to do was get rid of him. She said loudly, 'Excuse me, but you're in the wrong side of the cabin.'

The rumble, choked off, became a snort. His head fell sideways, burrowing into the pillow in a way that touched something deep inside her. Glowering, she said, 'Please wake up.'

No response, unless another snort could be called a response. Nicola leaned over, took the man by the shoulder and demanded, 'Wake up!'

His eyes flew open, he seized her by the wrists with such force that the whisky bottle was knocked off the bed and landed on her foot, and he said with a fury that took her aback, 'What the *hell* do you think you're doing?'

It took Nicola only a couple of seconds to recover, for the dig of his fingers in her wrists infuriated her, flooding her with energy. Bracing one knee against the side of the bed to avoid falling on top of him, she retorted, 'You're in my bed! And if that bottle's broken my toe, I'll sue you.' Her eyes, which were a lustrous brown and beautifully set under straight dark brows, suddenly widened in dismay. 'There's whisky running all over my foot,' she wailed. 'And my sandals are brand new...'

'What a waste of good liquor,' he commented, slurring the word 'waste' very slightly.

'*You* certainly don't need any more—you've had more than enough. Will you please get off my bed and out of my cabin?'

He released her wrists so quickly that she staggered backwards, and sank into the pillow again. 'I can't,' he said, closing his eyes. 'I'm far too drunk...as you so perspica—perspicaciously remarked.' And he smirked to himself in triumph as he finished his sentence.

Nicola fought for control. 'I find you less than amusing,' she said coldly, bending down to set the whisky bottle upright on the floor and screwing the cap on with vicious tightness. 'You found your way in here. You can find your way out.'

'Life is not always that s-simple.' He leered at her through one eye. 'You could pass up what's left in the bottle. No sense in saving that little bit. And you could introduce yourself.'

'*Out!*' she yelled.

He winced theatrically. 'There's no need to shout.'

Nicola gaped at him. Speaking to herself more than to him, she said, 'I don't usually shout. In fact, I never shout.'

'I have difficulty believing that.'

'I'll have you know I'm normally the most even-tempered of women!'

'Nonsense. You're a harridan. A virago. A shrew.'

'I'm *not*!'

'There you are, yelling again.'

Nicola swallowed hard. 'It's something about you,' she said icily. 'My grandmother always said I was a nice girl.'

'Nice is an awful word. As bland and tasteless as skimmed milk yoghurt. And just as dull.'

She gave him a withering look. 'Somehow this discussion seems to have shifted from whose bedroom you're in to skimmed milk yoghurt—very clever. But you *are* in the wrong bedroom and I want you to leave!'

Her voice had risen again. He said pacifyingly, 'Just leave me here to sleep it off, and then I'll go back to my place...I live next door,' he added unnecessarily. 'I must have come in here by mistake.'

'Probably because you couldn't face the mess of your place.'

'I need a good woman to look after me.' Another leer. 'You could apply—although you're kind of skinny, and I'm not sure about your haircut.'

Nicola, who thought of herself as slim rather than skinny and who liked her haircut, snapped back, 'You're living in the wrong century—women don't have to spend their lives cleaning up after men any more. Drunken men,' she added spitefully. 'Could we please stick to the point? I want you out of here. Now. And I do not want you to come back.'

'You've got two choices. Leave me here. Or join me.' He raised one brow. 'I'm not in any state to do you harm, believe me.'

His eyes were an astonishing sky-blue. You could lose yourself in those eyes, thought Nicola, and heard herself say, 'You've already made it clear that I don't appeal to you. So I'm safe on two counts, aren't I?' Then she caught herself and finished severely, 'There are indeed two choices, but not the ones you mentioned. Either you can remove yourself, or I shall remove you bodily.'

He favoured her with a lazy smile. 'How else would you remove me but bodily? This could be interesting. I think I'll stick around.'

Nicola felt a betraying warmth rise in her cheeks and tried to ignore it. She was five feet five and a half in her stockinged feet, and he had to be six feet tall. If upright. She remembered the swiftness with which he had seized her wrists and remembered, too, how this cabin was set off by itself, screened from both the house and the other cabins by a grove of pines and birches. She said bitterly, 'If this is how all you writers behave, I could be in for quite a summer.'

'I'm not a writer. I'm the caretaker, the groundsman, the gardener. Take your pick.'

Nicola gazed at him through narrowed eyes. That would explain the dirt on his clothes, and the heavy boots; but somehow she could not see someone with a jaw like his being the caretaker at an out-of-the-way writers colony in Newfoundland run by an elderly and eccentric widow.

He hiccupped with some gusto. 'I do wish you'd stop staring at me.'

'With pleasure! I'm going back to the house and telling Olivia I have no intentions of being the next-door neighbour of an alcoholic groundsman—I'm sure one of the other cabins is available. And...' she gave him a sweet smile '...I'm taking the remains of the whisky with me.'

Before he could reply she picked up the bottle, turned on her heel—the dry one—and stalked out of the bedroom. She pushed open the screen door with her suitcase and tramped through the woods towards the house, adrenalin still pumping through her veins so that she was blind to the beauty of the gently waving pine boughs and the curls of parchment-like bark on the birch trees. What an insufferable man! Nor could she possibly avoid him for the rest of the summer, not if he was the caretaker. Furthermore, she thought, adding to her list of grievances, she had liked the idea of being separate from the rest of the summer residents, and she had loved the low log cabin set in the trees on a bluff overlooking the blue waters of the bay. Water as blue as his eyes...

Nicola strode on, her case bumping against her knee. She was not in the habit of yelling at people, be they male or female, drunk or sober. Normally she kept her emotions well under control, the pattern of years. Normally she would have been calm, conciliatory, polite. Instead of which she had yelled like the harridan he had labelled her. Nor, she thought slowly, did she regret one word.

She gave herself a mental shake. The other cabins had looked very nice, and she would be happy wherever she was, because thanks to Olivia's sponsorship she had a whole summer to write her novel, a summer without financial worries or domestic cares, a summer spent on the rugged western shores of Newfoundland amid seabirds and wildflowers and ancient mountains. She was not going to let anyone ruin that for her, not even a drunken gardener who thought she was too skinny and her hair too short. Looking very fierce, she emerged from the trees on to the stretch of lawn that linked the main house with the other cabins.

Olivia's domain was called the Eyrie, because bald eagles nested in the hills that edged the shoreline. The main house was an exuberant conglomeration of Victorian bad taste, with cupolas, turrets, balconies, gingerbread carving and a great deal of wrought iron. It was painted two shades of green, with bright pink doors that clashed rather badly with the scarlet geraniums in the window boxes. I bet that man planted them, thought Nicola balefully, as she tramped up the front steps and into the coolness of the high-ceilinged entrance hall.

Olivia's office was on the right; Nicola tapped on the door. 'Come in,' fluted Olivia.

Olivia Elizabeth Vaughan Fitzrandolph had outlived three rich husbands, each of whom she had genuinely loved. At the funeral of the most recently deceased of these husbands she had informed her friends that three times a widow was enough for any woman, and since then had devoted herself with both imagination and verve to spending her various inheritances. The Eyrie was her latest project, for the benefit of indigent writers from Canada's eastern provinces; since there were very few writers living in this area who were not indigent, Olivia was swamped with applications, and Nicola had only got in at the last minute due to a cancellation. Due also to her subject matter, Nicola thought wryly as she smiled at her benefactor. For Nicola wanted to write romantic fiction, and, although Olivia loudly and publicly espoused the cause of the serious literary novel, there was nothing she liked better at the end of the day than to curl up with a good romance. 'After all,' she had said to Nicola at their preliminary interview, 'I've had three very happy marriages—so they must do some good!'

Now she smiled back at Nicola. 'All settled in?'

'Well, no. That's why I'm here.' Choosing her words with care, Nicola went on, 'When I went to my half of the cabin I discovered the caretaker, quite drunk, in my bed. He declined to remove himself. So I wondered if I could stay somewhere else?'

In quick succession amusement, dismay and calculation flitted across Olivia's face. 'Oh, dear,' she said. 'Let me think.'

Nicola looked away, discreetly not staring at Olivia's outfit. Olivia's first husband had been a rather famous fashion designer, and ever since then she had favoured the avant-garde; allied with the diamonds, sapphires and emeralds that were the combined legacy of all three husbands she could have cut a figure of fun were it not for the shrewdness and humour in her grey eyes. She was eccentric, she could afford to be eccentric, and she knew it.

She said slowly, 'All the cabins and the guest-rooms in the house are taken. There's only one other place, and that's a room in the attic, part of the servants quarters... are you sure he wouldn't move?'

'Quite sure.'

'It's very naughty of him,' Olivia said without much conviction. 'Leave your case here, Nicola, go up three flights and turn right—it's the only room up there that's been redecorated.'

Redecorated it might have been, but the little room poked under the eaves was stiflingly hot and graced with only one small window that had an uninspiring view of the next turret. The cabin that was rightfully Nicola's had many windows and a view of the bay; was she going to let a bottle of whisky and one man's rudeness immure her under the roof for the length of the summer? She went back downstairs and said, 'I much prefer the cabin.'

'Of course,' Olivia said soothingly. 'I'll go over and speak to Trent—he's normally a very reasonable man. Why don't you wait here?'

Why don't you fire him? thought Nicola, watching the retreat of Olivia's military-styled khaki jumpsuit, which boasted gold-encrested epaulettes and a stout canvas belt. Then she sat down for what she anticipated could be a lengthy wait. But in less than fifteen minutes Olivia returned. 'He's gone back to his own side,' she said. 'He promised there would be no repetition and he sends his apologies.'

All this had tripped so smoothly from Olivia's tongue that Nicola had little faith in either the promise or the apology. 'Thank you,' she said. 'I don't expect I'll see that much of him anyway.'

'Oh, he eats all his meals with us; I believe in demo-
cratic principles,' Olivia said vaguely. 'Dinner's at six,
I do find that writers get very hungry.' She sat down
behind her exquisite marquetry desk. 'Perhaps tomorrow evening we could have a little conference on your
first two chapters?'

Nicola nodded and made her escape. She had had
trouble with the first two chapters, especially with her
hero, and was coming to the conclusion that writing a
novel might be more difficult than she had expected.
She had met a highly successful author of romantic
fiction at a conference in St John's, and the idea of
writing a book each summer to pay for her university
education had been too good to pass up. After all, she
was studying English literature, she had always loved to
read, and she had written a series of short stories to
amuse her grandmother in the last few months of Gran's
life. Of course she could write a novel...

As she carried her suitcase between the trees for the
third time, Nicola pushed aside her worries about her
hero to wonder instead what Olivia could possibly have
said to have so swiftly removed Trent the gardener from
Nicola's side of the cabin to his own. Whatever it had
been, she hoped it would keep him there. She wanted
nothing to mar this gift of a summer.

As soon as she pushed open the screen door Nicola
knew her side of the cabin was empty. After the slightest
of hesitations she walked into the bedroom. The inden-
tation on the bed, the dirt on the white chenille bedspread, the sharp, medicinal odour of whisky all assailed
her senses. Dragging her eyes away from the bed, she
saw how her sandal was stained where the whisky had
spilled; suddenly she shivered, wondering if she was crazy
to isolate herself over here in this remote cabin with a
man who was an enigma to her. An unreliable man who

drank. A man for whom physically she was no match at all.

She sat down heavily on the bed, and found herself remembering how his hair had lain on the pillow. His hair-unlike the rest of him—had been beautifully clean.

Right on cue, she heard the groan of water pipes and then the loud swish of the shower from next door. The walls, she thought with a sinking of her heart, must be paper-thin; she would know his every movement. And he hers. Perhaps she had the answer to her own question. She *was* crazy to stay here for the sake of a view of the sea and the soft whisper of pine boughs against the roof.

Restlessly she got to her feet. The bedroom window was at the back of the cabin. Through the glass and the sun-dappled tree limbs she could see the gleam of blue water and a distant line of hills, and when she pushed the window up the wind stirred the flowered curtains and brought with it the mingled scent of resin and the sharp, clean tang of the sea. Her chin firmed and her mouth set in a resolute line. Trent whatever-his-name-was was not going to cheat her out of all this.

A hollow, metal booming came from next door. He had banged his elbow against the shower cubicle, she thought with intuitive accuracy, and across her truant brain flashed an image of him naked in the shower. Furious with herself, she blanked it out as swiftly as it had appeared, biting her lip. Her main motive in coming here was to write about an imaginary man and woman, about the kind of relationship she had always wanted and had never been able to keep, not to get involved with a real man. And certainly not with someone like Trent. Vindictively she hoped he was taking a cold shower to sober himself up. An ice-cold one.

As if he had read her thoughts, he burst into song. He was a baritone, rather a good one, singing in a language she decided was Spanish. Quite sure that the words, if translated into English, would make her blush, Nicola came to an instant decision: if she was to live her own life this summer, in spite of her difficult neighbour, she must start right now. She went into the living-room to get her suitcase and began to unpack, hanging her clothes in the bedroom cupboard, stacking her papers on the desk in the living-room that also held the computer she had been promised, all her movements quick and neat.

From next door she heard the creak of bedsprings and an exaggerated groan. His bedroom backed on to hers, she thought in horror, her hands stilling. And by the sound of it, his bed was against the wall. She could only pray he was not in the habit of bringing women to his cabin.

She could not bear that.

Stop it, she scolded herself. Stop it! And get to work.

She had a lot to do. Her first task was to familiarise herself with the computer, her second to transpose her two chapters on to a diskette; she had no time to worry about the problematic love-life of the man next door. She sat down at the desk, pleased to notice that through the window she had a delightful view of trees and sky, and switched on the power.

Two hours later a loud melodious chiming brought Nicola back to the world of reality. It must be the dinner bell, which Olivia had told her was the only way she could get a group of absent-minded writers together at one time. Pleased with her afternoon's work, pleased too with the silence from next door, Nicola carefully went through the steps to turn the computer off, then went into the bedroom and ran a comb through her hair. She was wearing slim-fitting blue jeans and a loose pink sweatshirt; because she was small-breasted, and perhaps because her more voluptuous sisters always wore sexy lace bras with plunging cleavages, Nicola rarely wore a bra. Her gleaming chestnut hair was very short, skilfully shaped so it clung to her head, the very boyishness of the cut emphasising the slender length of her neck and the size of her deep brown eyes. Her only jewellery was tiny gold earrings in the shape of scallop shells, a gift from her grandmother.

The meals were served buffet-style in an oak-panelled dining-room in the main house. Suddenly shy, for the room seemed full of people, none of whom she knew, all of whom knew each other, Nicola stopped at the doorway. Then Olivia emerged from the crowd, now dressed in a long flounced skirt and a lace-bedecked blouse. 'Come along and I'll introduce you to everyone,' she said.

Five minutes later Nicola was left with a bewildering array of faces and names and the certainty that she would never connect the two; but a sweet-faced young woman called Karen and a bearded young man whose name was Rafe ushered her towards the buffet, and as she heaped her plate with food she learned that Karen was a novelist and Rafe a poet. She began to relax. The salad bar would have done justice to any good hotel, and the shrimp casserole smelled delicious. She chose a hot roll from the basket, laughing at something Rafe had said, turned to find her seat at the long table where everyone ate, and came face to face with Trent.

Or rather, face to chest. Upright, he more than equalled her estimate of six feet; her eyes were level with the logo on his T-shirt. It was advertising a brand of local beer.

Nicola allowed her gaze to travel upwards, her nostrils tantalised by herbal soap and aftershave rather than whisky, to find his eyes a clear blue and not at all bloodshot, and a mocking smile on the sculpted lips. She said, with a coolness of which she was proud, 'What a remarkable recovery.'

'Amazing what a cold shower will do.'

Her eyes narrowed. Without consciously having thought about it at all, she announced, 'You weren't drunk! You stank of whisky because you'd spilled it all over your shirt. Deliberately. No accident.'

'So you have brains as well as beauty.'

Her guess, a shot in the dark, had been right on target. Furthermore, he had already made it quite clear that he did not find her beautiful. Aware that Rafe had faded tactfully out of earshot, she flashed, 'You don't want me living next door to you, do you?'

'Got it in one.'

Nicola, by no means a violent woman, was visited by the sudden urge to decorate his T-shirt with green salad and shrimp casserole and see if that would wipe the infuriating smile from his mouth. 'You're stuck with me,' she said. 'Too bad.'

'We'll see about that . . . my name, by the way, is Trent Livingstone.'

He had not only been aware of her impulse, he had been amused by it, she could tell. This did nothing to improve her temper. 'Nicola Shea,' she responded, biting off the words.

'Please feel free to yell,' he said amiably. 'They say repression's very bad for you.'

The image Nicola had always had of herself as calm and composed skidded further off centre. Trent Livingstone might be large and attractive, but he was still only a man; how could he change her behaviour so drastically? She said flatly, 'How about if you leave me alone, and I'll leave you alone? Is that a deal?'

'I'm not into making deals—I value my privacy too much. And now I really think you should go and eat your dinner, it's getting cold.' He finished blandly, 'I do hope you like Spanish bar songs, I'm afraid my repertoire is a little limited.'

'I hope the shower was glacial,' she snapped vindictively, knowing that in five minutes she would think of any number of wittier replies. She turned away, saw an empty seat next to Rafe and hurriedly sat down. Rafe, who would probably never be a really good poet because he was too nice a man, ignored her flushed cheeks and said easily, 'Are you from Newfoundland, Nicola?'

Still breathing rather fast, Nicola acknowledged, 'I grew up in St John's.' St John's was the capital of Newfoundland, on the eastern coast. 'And I've been going to Memorial University for the last two years...mmm, delicious salad.'

Karen, sitting across from them, joined in the conversation. But as they talked about restaurants and the regional novel, about recipes and postmodernist poetry, Nicola's thoughts churned away beneath the surface. Trent Livingstone had not even bothered to deny her accusation. He had blatantly deceived her, made a fool of her, and all because he did not want her living next door. She should have poured the remains of the bottle of whisky all over him. She should have dumped a bucket of cold water on him. Spanish bar songs, indeed!

But why was he so adamantly against sharing the cabin? Did he have something against her personally, or would he have hated anyone who disturbed the privacy he so obviously craved?

She had no idea of the answers to these questions. However, she did wish with all her heart that Trent were living anywhere other than next door to her.

CHAPTER TWO

NICOLA took her last mouthful of the shrimp casserole, which had deserved more attention than she had paid it, and tried to concentrate on what Rafe was saying about the deplorable state of the market for poetry. Then Karen said in a non-committal voice, 'Suzie's just come in.'

Rafe winced. When he looked up, Nicola would have had to be blind not to see the emotion that flared in his face. So Rafe was in love with Suzie, and not altogether happily, she thought, glancing across the room to see who had inspired this emotion.

It was no trouble to find her. For Suzie was beautiful, a dark gypsy of a woman in a full red skirt nipped to a tiny waist, and a white peasant blouse that left little to the imagination; a glittering fringed scarf was artfully draped over one shoulder, and gold hoops swayed in her ears. Nicola felt her heart clench with an old pain, for Suzie had what both of Nicola's sisters had; that elusive, sensual quality called sex appeal, that highly charged femininity that attracted men like moths to a flame. Nicola, to her cost, knew about sex appeal. She had lost two men to it, one to her sister Gayle, the other to her sister Cheryl.

Somehow she was not at all surprised to see Suzie sink gracefully into the chair next to Trent Livingstone and toss off a remark that made him laugh. Rafe addressed himself to his salad, cutting a radish in half with a force that made both pieces fly on to the tablecloth. So Suzie was probably sharing Trent's bed, thought Nicola, which would explain Rafe's unhappiness and Trent's reluctance to have an unknown female lying on the other side of the wall. Trent had wasted a bottle of whisky, she thought grimly; she, Nicola, would flee to the attic room at the first sign of any lovemaking in that creaking bed so close to hers.

She said with determined brightness, 'I caught sight of chocolate cheesecake, didn't I? Are you going to have dessert, Rafe? What about you, Karen?'

'I shouldn't,' Karen groaned. 'I really shouldn't. I love writing, I can't imagine doing anything else, but it does mean you spend a great deal of your life sitting. Which in my case is having a deleterious effect on the hips.' She grinned at Nicola. 'On the other hand, chocolate might inspire the scene I'm working on—get it out of the doldrums. Worth trying, don't you agree, Rafe?'

Rafe managed a smile. 'You could bring me a piece,' he suggested, stabbing at his last piece of lettuce.

Karen and Nicola headed for the far end of the buffet. 'That bitch Suzie,' hissed sweet-faced Karen. 'I could kill her. She's not the slightest bit interested in Rafe—he's far too nice for her. But she has to keep him on the hook—I think she likes to see him suffer.'

Nicola, who had no problem believing every word of this, said indiscreetly, 'Trent Livingstone should be her match.'

Karen gave her a curious look. 'Of course, you're living next door to him, aren't you? Oh, Trent's all right, he can look after himself. It's Rafe I'm worried about.'

So what did that mean? Nicola wondered, cutting a very generous slab of cheesecake for Rafe, and knowing she was too proud to ask. Was Karen in love with Rafe, who was in love with Suzie? Who was probably not in love with Trent, but equally probably lusted after him. The Suzies of this world loved only themselves, she thought glumly, and cut an even larger piece of cheesecake for herself. She had come here to get away from all these entanglements. To write about them. Not to see them going on in front of her eyes.

As if to contradict her, Karen hissed, 'Oops, here comes Suzie—you haven't met her, have you?'

Suzie, hips swinging, was walking towards them. Karen said clearly, 'Suzie, this is Nicola Shea, who's just joined us. Nicola, Suzie Donovan.'

Suzie's eyes, green as a cat's, flicked over Nicola without interest. She held out a languid hand, said, 'Hello,' with a minimal smile and continued on her way.

Karen said ruefully, 'Don't take it personally—Suzie's not interested in women.'

A more accurate statement would be that Suzie did not see Nicola as any competition, thought Nicola with a matching twist of her lips. Carrying the two plates, she headed back to Rafe.

But the cheesecake was delicious enough to take her mind off Suzie, and was followed by excellent coffee. Karen pushed back her chair, a militant light in her eye. 'Back to the grind,' she said. 'See you tomorrow, Nicola... Do you play tennis? There are courts behind the house.'

They agreed to a game at four the following afternoon, and Karen left. Rafe shot a venomous glance down the table, where Suzie had draped herself over Trent's arm, and said with faint desperation, 'Would you like to go for a walk, Nicola? I'll show you the path to the next cove.'

Nicola knew why he wanted her company: she was a new ear into which he could pour his misery. Too kind-hearted to refuse him—for she had been in his shoes, and knew how painfully they could pinch—she said truthfully, 'I love walking, and I'd like to get my bearings here. Can you wait until I get my sneakers?'

A dirt road led past the Eyrie to the shore, where small waves washed on to the pebble beach and seaweed swirled around the pilings of the wharf. A couple of flat-bottomed dories were moored there, their pointed prows slapping against the water. 'Trent keeps the oars and the lifejackets if you ever want to take one of the dories out,' Rafe said.

Nicola had had a terror of the water and of boats ever since the accident in which both her parents had drowned. She looked away from the cheerfully painted dories. 'I don't expect I'll have the time,' she said.

But Rafe was not listening. 'Before Trent came, Suzie used to spend all her time with me. She's a poet too, you see, so we have a lot in common.' He tugged at his moustache, which was as tidily clipped as his beard and his black hair. 'I don't know what she sees in Trent.'

Nicola knew exactly what she saw. Trent spelled danger; raw masculinity; sex. Nicola could remember with embarrassing clarity how the beer cans on his T-shirt had hugged the flat muscles of his chest, how the light had caught the dusting of fair hair on his forearms, how difficult it had been to drag her gaze away from the piercing blue of his eyes. Oh, yes, she knew what Suzie saw in Trent Livingstone. She said diplomatically, 'Perhaps she'll grow tired of him.'

'A meeting of intellects is basic to any relationship,' Rafe said earnestly. 'He's just a gardener, after all.'

I wouldn't be too sure of that.

The thought had popped into Nicola's head unasked, and slowly she turned it over in her mind. It was hard to visualise a man like Trent being satisfied for long with weeding perennial borders and trimming privet hedges. 'How long has he been here?' she asked.

'Less than two weeks. Turned up one day out of the blue a week after the rest of us arrived. Keeps pretty much to himself, mind you.'

They had been following a trail through the trees at the far end of the beach, a trail that now opened out on a promontory overlooking the bay. 'How beautiful!' Nicola exclaimed spontaneously.

Rafe, the poet, looked at the foam-edged cove, the wind-ruffled water and the looming hills on the far shore with a noticeable lack of enthusiasm. 'I suppose it is,' he said. 'Suzie and I came here once. She said...' And he was off.

Nicola listened as patiently as she could, drinking in the evening's serenity, her pleasure intensified when she sighted a pair of eagles roosting in the trees further down the shore. When Rafe finally paused for breath at the end of a long list of grievances, she said, 'I don't think Suzie will ever be the type to be content with only one man, Rafe...Karen looks much nicer to me.'

'But it's Suzie I'm in love with!' Rafe said, shocked. 'Anyway, Karen's married.'

And what was Nicola to reply to that? She had been in love, twice, and neither time had she been able to hold on to the man of her choice. 'Shall we go back?' she said. 'I'd like to finish typing my second chapter tonight.'

Rafe fastened his eyes on her face; not unkindly, Nicola thought they were rather like a spaniel's eyes in their combination of dolour and appeal. He said, 'I don't think you understand.'

Discovering she did not want to share the story of her own two truncated romances with him, she replied as gently as she could, 'Have you tried putting any of this in your poetry?'

'I've got a whole binder of poems.' With the first glimmer of humour he had shown, he added, 'But I call her Sylvie in the poems. Suzie isn't a very romantic name.'

Nicola laughed, deciding there was hope for Rafe after all, and started back along the path. When he left her by the head of the trail that led to her cabin, he leaned forward and kissed her cheek. 'Thanks for listening,' he said.

She patted him on the arm and wondered what it would have been like growing up with a brother like Rafe instead of two sisters like Gayle and Cheryl. Not that she saw that much of her sisters now that they had moved to the bright lights of Halifax. 'You're welcome,' she said. 'See you tomorrow.'

The little clearing at the end of the trail was bathed in the golden light of evening, and the other half of the cabin was empty. Wishing with an intensity that rather shocked her that it would remain empty permanently, Nicola walked behind the cabin. The same gold light was reflected on the bay and the plaintive cry of a gull drifted through the trees. It was so peaceful when she was here alone...

She wandered inside, latching the door behind her, went into the bathroom to brush her teeth, and met her eyes in the mirror. Her hair was so short that its natural curl was hardly in evidence. As for the rest, she saw a straight nose, an ordinary chin, a slender neck disappearing into the loose folds of the pink sweater. There was none of the come-hither look that Suzie flaunted with such confidence and ease, only a deep wariness in the lustrous brown eyes.

What she did not see was the sweep of flawless, creamy skin from cheekbone to chin, the entrancing tilt of the brown eyes with their thick dark lashes, or the generous curve of her forehead under the sleek chestnut hair, which under the light gleamed like a helmet. She was blind to those, for no one had ever pointed them out to her. 'She's the plain one,' Gran had been apt to confide to her friends of her youngest granddaughter; and later, when Nicola was a teenager, 'Of course I never have any trouble with boys as far as Nicola is concerned.' A theatrical sigh. 'Not like the other two.'

Nicola heaved a sigh herself, rinsed her toothbrush and pulled a face at herself in the mirror. You're wasting time, she told herself firmly. You came here to write a novel, a novel that will sell and earn you enough money so you can go back to university. So get on with it.

Taking her own advice, Nicola turned on the computer and worked for two hours, until she was well into her third chapter. Ten-thirty and not a sound from next door, she thought with considerable satisfaction. It was going to be all right after all having Trent for a neighbour—she'd have lots of time to work. Stretching lazily to ease her shoulder muscles, she decided to have a shower.

The shower cubicle appeared to have been designed with a child in mind. A small child. Nicola could see why Trent had banged his elbow. Nor was the water pressure up to much, she thought, scrubbing her hair under the dribbles emerging from the shower head, and trying to avoid knocking her own elbows. She felt cheated, because she loved a hot shower, although it was a minor complaint when she considered all the other benefits the Eyrie was offering her.

Eventually, dried and powdered, she snuggled into the three-quarter bed. The sheets smelled fresh, as though they had been dried outdoors in the summer wind, and the lightweight duvet was very comfortable. Thinking about her heroine, whose name was Maryanne, Nicola drifted off to sleep.

The noise that woke her sounded like a gunshot. Terrified, her heart racing, Nicola sat up in bed. Then she heard the thud of footsteps through the thin wall, and reason took over from panic. Trent. Trent had come home and banged the screen door.

She glanced at the illuminated dial of her clock radio. Twelve-fifty, it said; she had been asleep for well over an hour. Very cautiously, so as not to make any noise, she lay down again, pulling the duvet up to her chin. Water ran in the bathroom next door. A cupboard door creaked open, then shut, and she heard two thumps as Trent presumably dropped his boots on the floor. From three feet up, Nicola thought furiously. He not only was making no effort to be quiet, he was deliberately being as noisy as he could. But to her everlasting gratitude there was no sound of conversation, no feminine laughter; he was alone. Nor, she thought with a wry twist of her mouth, was he singing. Something else to be grateful for.

So close she could have sworn he was in the same room with her, she heard the scrape of his zipper and the small intimate sounds of him getting undressed. Her cheeks grew warm, her eyes wide in the darkness. The bed-springs squeaked, and squeaked again as he settled himself. His voice—warm, amused—said, 'Goodnight, Nicola.' Then silence.

Rigid under the duvet, Nicola stared up at the ceiling, her lips tightly compressed to prevent herself from spitting out a response. How dared he purposefully wake her up and then have the gall to wish her goodnight? The last thing she would give him was the satisfaction of knowing he had succeeded, that she was lying wide awake less than six feet away from him; it was a strange feeling, to know he was so close, only divided from her by a thin wall of boards and gyprock.

Divided by more than a wall, she fumed. He had to be the rudest man, the most inconsiderate and egotistical man she had ever met. He did not want her next door. So he would condemn her to a stuffy little room in the attic for the whole summer just so he could get his own way. Well, they'd see about that. She was not so easily routed.

But as the clock counted off the minutes one by one and a slow, rhythmic breathing wafted through the wall, Nicola's resolve weakened. She needed her sleep. She had only two months to get her novel in shape, so she was going to have to work very hard all summer, and to work that hard she would have to feel rested and full of energy. If every night she was to be woken up by Trent Livingstone, her task would be much more difficult.

She had not bargained for this.

Resolutely she closed her eyes. He was not going to ruin her summer. He was *not*.

But it was past two-thirty before she managed to fall asleep again, and she was dead to the world when a fist banged on the wall of her bedroom and a cheerful baritone voice called, 'Time to wake up, Nicola—breakfast in twenty minutes!'

Nicola, woken from a confused dream of a poetry reading at which Cheryl was performing the Dance of the Seven Veils, sat bolt upright. Her eyes were burning and she could remember every long minute she had lain awake in the middle of the night. Instantly and thoroughly outraged, she leaped out of bed, hauled her housecoat over her head, and lunged for the door. She stamped down the steps and up Trent's steps in her bare feet and yanked his door open. He was standing, dressed in faded jeans and a cotton shirt, by the stone fireplace.

After letting the spring slam the door shut as loudly as it had shut in the middle of the night, she cried, 'This has got to stop!'

'Really, Nicola, didn't your mother teach you to knock before you burst into a strange man's room? I sleep in the nude, you know.'

So when he had been lying six feet away from her he had been naked under the sheets; a deep, inward shiver rippled along her nerves. Praying that he had not sensed it, she announced with renewed anger, 'Then I'm glad you had the foresight to put some clothes on before you so kindly woke me up. For the second time in the last twelve hours.'

'Rather a pity that *you* did.' He surveyed her lazily from top to toe. Her Hawaiian housecoat, a gift from Gayle, left only her hands and feet uncovered, although beneath the orange and yellow flowers scattered over the bodice her breast rose and fell; her hair, damp when she had gone to bed, stood up around her head in tiny spikes, and her cheeks were bright pink. He drawled, 'As for stopping, why, I've scarcely started.'

'I shall tell Olivia what you're doing!'

'Feel free. Although Olivia is not the type of woman to appreciate a whiner.'

He was right, of course. Almost choking with indignation, Nicola sputtered, 'You're deliberately harassing me. Without the slightest consideration for my feelings——'

'That's where you're wrong,' Trent said soothingly. 'Do you really want to be next door when I bring Suzie back with me some night?'

She did not. In fact, the mere thought of it caused a turmoil of emotion in her breast. 'So all this is for my own good, is it?' she retorted nastily, raising her chin. 'Listen to me, Trent Livingstone. If you can't keep your hands off Suzie—and I'm not surprised, she looks exactly your type—then *you* go to Suzie's cabin instead of bringing her here. And in future leave me alone!'

'So you've got claws,' he mused, rubbing his chin. 'There's nothing wrong with Suzie.'

With the strong feeling that the whole interview was slipping away from her, Nicola said, 'I did not come here to discuss Suzie. I came to ask you to exercise a minimal degree of politeness and consideration.'

'You look a little tired—didn't you sleep well?'

Nicola let out her breath in a long sigh and decided to change tactics; losing her temper did not seem to be getting her very far. 'This is all very childish, Trent,' she said in a calm, reasonable voice that her sisters would have recognised. 'Please leave me alone. I've only got the summer to work on my book, I've got to get a job in the fall, so two months is all I have . . . please don't spoil it for me.'

He said kindly, 'If you could coax a tear or two? That's a sure-fire way of softening a man's heart, so I've heard.'

Nicola stared at him in silence. Then she said, 'I see. It's war, isn't it, Trent? Open war. You against me.'

'No holds barred,' he said agreeably.

'Fine.' She gave him a dazzling smile. 'May the best woman win.'

'Oh, I don't think that will be the outcome.' He raised his brow. 'By the way, have your tried the shower yet, Nicola?'

'Yes,' she said shortly. 'It doesn't work very well.'

'That's because I borrowed a part from it. Rather an essential part.' He glanced out of the window. 'The bay's warming up quite nicely, though—you can always go for a swim.'

If there was one thing certain, it was that Nicola would not be going for a swim. Her fear of the water had proscribed swimming years ago. Trying hard to think of a suitable retort, she heard, through the screen, the breakfast bell chime sweetly six times. 'Dammit,' Nicola exploded, 'now I'll be late,' and whirled on her heel.

'I'll save you an egg,' said Trent.

'I'll make you sorry for this,' she choked, and almost fell out of the door. Back in her cabin she got dressed with furious haste. He had won another round. Hands down.

Whatever happened, he must not win the next.

Despite its bad beginning the day proceeded calmly. Trent stayed away from the cabin and Nicola pushed ahead with chapter three; she had given Olivia the first two chapters after breakfast, and had not mentioned the shenanigans of her neighbour. Who, she had noticed sourly, had been neatly appropriated by Suzie at the far end of the breakfast table. At four Nicola played three sets of vigorous tennis with Karen, whose gentle demeanour masked a strong competitive streak, and had another unsatisfactory shower; for the first time in her life she wished she knew something about plumbing, so that she could have reappropriated the missing part.

After dinner, which was dominated by an impassioned discussion on copyright, Nicola headed for Olivia's office. Olivia, she now knew, did not exercise any editorial capacity with the other writers, but because Olivia loved romantic novels, considering herself something of an expert on them, she was keenly interested in the progress of Nicola's. As Nicola hesitated for a moment outside the door, she discovered she was nervous about Olivia's opinion, a lot more nervous than she would have anticipated.

She braced herself, knocked on the oak panels and walked in. Olivia was adjusting the window, a south-facing window where old-fashioned roses nodded heavy pink heads against the panes. 'Close the door,' said Olivia, 'and sit down. I love the scent of the old roses, don't you? My second husband was a great rose grower.' And she gave a sigh of pleasurable melancholy.

But when she sat down at the desk, a little heap of typescript in front of her, she was all business. Tapping one finger on the manuscript, the emerald on her knuckle winking malevolently at Nicola, she said, 'Nicola, I'm going to be very blunt. There's some good writing here, no question of that—your descriptions are fine, and there's a real sense of place. But your hero and heroine are all wrong. Have you ever been in love?'

'Yes!' Nicola replied, stung.

'I don't get any sense from your writing that you've ever loved a man heart, soul and body...are you a virgin?'

Nicola sat up a little straighter. 'I don't think that's any of your business,' she said warmly.

'So you are...I rather thought so.' Olivia gave a most unladylike snort. 'Don't look so shocked, child. There's a look about you, an untouched look—a dead giveaway to an old woman like me. I suppose I can't suggest that for the sake of art you go out and lose that virginity...? Hmm, I thought not.'

'I trust you didn't put me next door to Trent with that in mind,' Nicola snapped.

Olivia's grey eyes sharpened with genuine interest. 'Why, is he making advances? How fascinating!'

'No! He's not.' Not to her. He had other prey to pursue. Besides, Nicola thought, acknowledging how the word still rankled, he thought she was too skinny.

'Pity,' said Olivia. 'Now, if I were fifty years younger, neither you nor Suzie would stand a chance.' She put her head to one side. 'An extraordinarily good poet,

Suzie; she'll go far. But her morals are what you might call flexible.'

'I'm sure you didn't ask me here to discuss Suzie's morals.'

Olivia gave an undignified cackle. 'It would be a short discussion.' Still grinning, she rattled the papers. 'Now, back to your hero. He's wishy-washy, Nicola. Inoffensive. I can't imagine him doing anything daring. Anything outrageous. *I* wouldn't fall in love with him.'

'But I like him!'

'Oh, he's likeable, he's nice. Too nice. That's the whole trouble. Did you ever hear of a nice pirate captain? Or a nice Arabian sheikh? I know your hero's Canadian, but that doesn't mean he's got to be dull. I married three Canadians, and not one of them was dull. Was the man you were in love with dull?'

Trent had also allied niceness with dullness. 'No! Of course not. At least I don't think so. There were two of them,' Nicola said incoherently. 'I don't *know* any Arabian sheikhs.'

'Then you must use your imagination,' Olivia said briskly. 'That's exactly what's wrong with your heroine; she needs to loosen up. She's far too prim. Imagine yourself being kidnapped on a pure white stallion, whisked to a tent in the desert and seduced on a silken couch...then transpose it to a Newfoundland fishing village—that's all you've got to do. Simple!'

'Simple,' Nicola echoed in a hollow voice.

Olivia stood up. 'I would suspect it's not only your heroine who needs to loosen up,' she remarked. 'It would do you all the good in the world to fall in love, Nicola. Really in love.'

'I don't want to! Not again.'

'You don't have to tell me that, it shows in your writing—you're fighting emotion every step of the way.'

Olivia put her head to one side. 'If you had to use one word to describe yourself, what would it be?'

'Ordinary,' said Nicola.

'Pooh!' Olivia replied. 'Under that sweatshirt I would suspect you're hiding an admirable figure. Add to that eyes of rare beauty, a truly elegant haircut and the choirboy purity of your face—dynamite. Pure dynamite.' She pushed the manuscript across the desk. 'Well, I've said enough. More than enough, probably—I never did learn tact. Come back in a couple of weeks when you've made some revisions.'

The interview as patently over. Nicola got to her feet, picked up the papers and left without a word. Her thoughts were confused, her throat felt tight and she very badly wanted to cry. Praying she would not meet anyone between here and the cabin, she walked down the corridor, through the front door past the red geraniums and down the path between twin rows of gaudy petunias. She had never liked petunias.

Crossing the neatly mown grass—mowed by Trent, she supposed—she decided with the blackness of despair that she was a fool. Whatever had given her the idea that she could write a publishable novel, one the editors would like and the readers would buy? Sure, she had done exceptionally well in all her English courses, but that was no guarantee that she could write. Obviously. Look what Olivia had just said.

Your hero and heroine are all wrong...

The pine trees enclosed her, the needles brushing her face. She should leave right now, she thought, feeling the tears sting her eyes. She was wasting Olivia's money and her own time. She'd be better off working in a shop in St John's and saving every penny she could than kidding herself that she could earn her way with her imagination. Because her hero, whose name was Jonathan, was a long way from an Arabian sheikh...

She stopped by the side of the trail, absently breaking a twig from the nearest bough and pulling off the needles, one by one. She had made her hero a composite of George and Allan, the two men she had been in love with, she thought with coruscating honesty. George, who had fallen for Gayle. And Allan, who had run straight into Cheryl's open arms.

She *had* been in love with them, hadn't she?

She stripped another twig from the tree. According to Olivia, she, Nicola, had never been in love. Basing her opinion on less than forty pages of typescript, Olivia had divined some lack in Nicola, something missing. What had she implied? That Nicola, like her heroine, needed to loosen up. Needed, Nicola thought viciously, to lose her virginity for the sake of art.

Her fingers were sticky with pine gum. She gazed at them as if she had never seen them before. Slender, attractive fingers, bare of rings, with clean, unpolished nails. She had noticed Suzie's fingers last night when she had been introduced to her in front of the desserts. They had been dirty, decorated with cheap rings, the scarlet nail polish chipped and flaking. Was that what it took?

I'm me, she thought with a touch of desperation. I can only be me. I've never been seduced on a silken couch. I've never been seduced anywhere. Once George had met Gayle, and Allan Cheryl, she had been forgotten.

And suddenly the tears overflowed, dripping from Nicola's lashes to run down her cheeks. She began to run, dashing the branches aside with her hands, her vision blurred. She wanted to be in her own cabin, in the security of four walls. Alone. Then maybe she could decide what she was going to do.

Her footsteps soundless on the springy turf, she burst out of the trees, sprinted across the clearing and ran lightly up the steps. She was like an animal hiding to lick its wounds, she thought frantically as she tugged at the screen door. She had expected a critique on her book and had heard, instead, a critique on her life, a résumé of all that was wrong with it.

Because she was blinded by tears, she tripped over the top step as she shoved the wooden door inwards, and stumbled headlong into the living-room. Struggling for balance, her manuscript cascading to the floor, she saw in front of her, the image imprinted in her brain like a photograph, a pair of jeans-clad legs ending in work boots. Work boots that she recognised all too well. With a shocked gasp she stood upright and met Trent's eyes. For the first time since she had met him, he looked visibly disconcerted.

For Nicola it was a classic case of the straw that broke the camel's back. Swept by a surge of pure rage, stronger than anything she had ever felt before, Nicola stood very still, her fists clenched at her sides. Olivia had told her to loosen up; loosen up she would. 'Get out,' she ordered in a voice she scarcely recognised as her own.

Her cheeks were streaked with tears, her lashes wet with tears. Trent took a step towards her and said abruptly, 'What's wrong, Nicola?'

'I said get out!'

'Not until you tell me what's wrong—why you're crying.'

'I'm not crying—I never cry!'

'Just like you never yell,' he said drily.

Fighting for breath, she seethed, 'What's wrong is my affair. Not yours.' She flung one arm towards the door in a gesture whose vehemence, even through the red mists of rage, rather horrified her. 'Get out, Trent. If you value living.'

It should have been a ludicrous statement, but somehow was not. He did not laugh, and not even a shadow of amusement crossed his face. Instead Nicola saw the sharpening of interest, an interest she could only suppose was in her behaviour, overlaid with a concern she would have sworn was genuine. Both of these reactions further enraged her. 'Don't you dare look at me as though I'm something under a microscope,' she hissed.

His gaze locked with hers, he circled her until he was standing by the door. Then he said, 'I want to know what upset you.'

She advanced on him, her eyes brilliant with unshed tears. 'Upset?' she repeated sarcastically. 'Whatever gave you that idea? I've only been told that my book is no good and my life is on a par with it—that's all. Nothing to get upset about. Just a minor setback.'

'Nicola——'

Suddenly all the anger of years burst into flame. Anger against Allan and George for deserting her. Against Cheryl and Gayle for being who they were. Against Gran for dismissing her as plain. Against her parents for drowning in front of her eyes and leaving her an orphan. Almost paralysed with fury, she croaked, 'I don't want your concern. Or your interest, Trent Livingstone. I don't want anything to do with you. *I* want to be left alone just as much as you do. So why don't you get the *hell* out of here and we'll agree to ignore each other for the rest of the summer? *Out!*'

His eyes narrowed. It was quite plain he was not intimidated by her rage; equally plain that her words had made an impact on him. With a strange note in his voice he said, 'OK—I'm leaving. But don't count on my not coming back. When and how it suits me.'

'Privacy!' she spat. 'That's what we both want. Think about it, Trent, and stay away.'

He pushed the door open with the flat of his hand. Then, as if he had thought the better of it, he let it bang shut. In one quick stride he closed the gap between himself and Nicola, grasped her by the shoulders, bent his head and kissed her open mouth.

The flame of rage in Nicola leaped to mingle with a flame of desire so fierce, so primitive, and so unexpected that it shook her to the roots of her being. The grip of his hands, the burning heat of his mouth seared every nerve in her body; when he released her as suddenly as he had seized her she had to stagger to keep her balance, and her eyes were liquid with emotion. She could not have spoken to save her soul.

Trent drew in a long breath; had Nicola not been shocked to the core she might have noticed that he, too, looked as though solid ground had just shifted beneath his feet. 'Well... that was quite a surprise,' he said, and it would have taken an ear more acute than Nicola's to have labelled the emotion in his voice. 'You look so prim and proper in your pink sweater, with your haircut that could be a boy's—and one kiss makes a lie out of it all.'

He was waiting for her to say something, the pulse throbbing under the tanned skin at the open neck of his shirt. But Nicola, who for the first time in her life had discovered passion, was still speechless. He added with a fiendish grin, running his fingers through his blond hair, 'If you should happen to need anything—anything at all—in the night, just bang on the wall. I'm a very light sleeper.'

This time, when he pushed the door open, he vanished through it. Nicola, rooted to the spot, heard him jump to the ground and then the soft pad of footsteps across the grass.

Going to visit Suzie, whispered a nasty little voice in her ear. He knows Suzie's passionate.

I don't give a damn where he's gone, thought Nicola. With hands that were not quite steady, she latched the inner wooden door, drew all the curtains in the living-room, and bent to pick up the scattered pages of chapters one and two. The page that had ended on top was one in which Maryanne, the heroine, and Jonathan, the hero, had had a disagreement. In the margin in violet ink Olivia had scrawled, 'This is like a ladies' tea party, little cucumber sandwiches and fussy cakes—put boxing gloves on them, Nicola!'

And Nicola, still on fire with a mixture of emotions she had no desire whatever to categorise, picked up the challenge. All right, she thought, turning on the computer and automatically keying to the right file. If you want boxing gloves, Olivia, you'll get them. With a vengeance.

She began to type, slowly at first, then her fingers flying over the keys. She typed for over an hour, and at the end of it she had six pages where previously she had had one. She printed them, tore the last page out of the machine, and switched on the lamp by the armchair to read them.

The words were invested with energy; they carried her along with their own momentum; she was astounded that she had written them. Maryanne had yelled at Jonathan. Jonathan had yelled back. Maryanne was wittier than she had ever been before, and Jonathan more masculine. More arrogant. More...interesting.

Slowly Nicola reread the scene, knowing instinctively that Olivia would approve of it, and that Olivia had been right to criticise its predecessor. She was halfway down

the fourth page when her breath caught in her throat
and her gaze was riveted to a single word. Instead of
typing Jonathan she had typed Trent. Who had run his
fingers through his blond hair.

Jonathan's hair was black.

She put the page down with hands that were unsteady,
as all the implications of those two small slips tumbled
into her tired brain. It wasn't Jonathan's voice that she
had heard as she had typed that scene, it was Trent's.
The arrogance, the masculinity, the ruthlessness were all
Trent's.

A classic Freudian slip. And she had made two of
them.

I'm not attracted to Trent, she told herself frantically.
I hate him!

Sure, came an answering voice, full of mockery.

I do! He's been nothing but a nuisance, playing silly
tricks on me, acting like a ten-year-old.

Ten-year-olds don't kiss the way Trent kisses.
Remember?

Of course she remembered—how could she have forgotten? I suppose I should be grateful that Jonathan
didn't kiss Maryanne, she thought miserably. Then I
would have been in trouble.

In trouble? queried the nasty little voice. The man's
rescuing your book, for goodness' sake. Making it come
alive. Don't talk to me about trouble.

I'm writing this book, Nicola replied with great
dignity. I'll thank you to remember that. Now, go away!

She went back to the computer, scrolled to the
offending page, and changed Trent to Jonathan and
blond to black, by which time she had convinced herself
that the slips had occurred merely because she was tired
and upset, and for no other reason. Then she turned off
the machine and went to bed.

CHAPTER THREE

AT SEVEN-THIRTY the next morning Nicola woke up. Her first sensation was of rain pattering on the roof, a gentle, soothing sound that could easily have lulled her back to sleep. But the breakfast bell would ring in half an hour, and she had to have a shower. The second, more uncomfortable sensation that jerked her fully awake was the utter silence from next door.

She had not heard Trent come back last night. He had not banged the door, or dropped his shoes, or called goodnight. Neither had she heard him get up this morning.

She strained her ears for any noises from the adjoining rooms. Nothing. Not even the steady rhythm of his breathing.

There was only one conclusion she could come to. He was not there. Without stopping to think, she raised her fist and banged on the wall.

No response. No amused baritone voice saying, 'Good morning, Nicola.' No creaking of the bed springs as he turned over. Just the same dead silence.

Her thoughts carried her inexorably forward. He had taken her advice and stayed at Suzie's for the night. So it *had* been concern she had seen in his face last night before that single, devastating kiss had rocked her world; he must have felt guilty, deciding he had harassed her too much, and that they could live amicably side by side in the same building and give each other ample privacy.

It had all worked out as she had wished. Why then did she have this sick feeling in the pit of her stomach?

Not wanting to answer her own question, Nicola got out of bed. The bay was not visible through the bedroom window, for the trees were wreathed in a fine misty rain; the pine boughs were silvered with dampness and the air was still.

I sleep in the nude, Trent had said. So, Nicola was sure, would Suzie. Her mind flinching away from the image of them in each other's arms, she made her bed with hasty movements and went to the bathroom. But when she turned on the shower, the pipes gave a pained wheeze and three drops of water landed on her head. With an impatient grimace she turned the hot and cold taps full on. One more drop. She turned them off, then on again. Nothing.

Into her mind dropped the image of Trent standing in her living-room when she had burst in the door last night. He had, she remembered, looked disconcerted. In the ensuing argument it had not occurred to her to ask him what he had been doing. Why he had been trespassing.

She now knew. He had done something to the shower so it did not work at all.

You've gone too far this time, Trent Livingstone, she thought grimly. I'm going to see Olivia right now, and if that makes me a whiner, then a whiner I am. And Olivia's going to pay for a plumber to fix the shower and a locksmith to fit a key in my door. So you can't come in here again, uninvited.

This decision made her feel minimally less unhappy. She pulled on a pale yellow sweatsuit and her sandals, resolutely ignoring the whisky stain on the left one, grabbed her jacket and left the cabin. The rain drifted against her cheeks, as cool and soft as the brush of fingers, while the air was rich with the scent of ferns and leaf-mould. But Nicola closed her mind to the morning's elusive beauty, nursing her anger, holding it tightly in her chest. For under the anger lay hurt, hurt that Trent's concern last night had, after all, been no more genuine than a counterfeit bill; when she had—literally—fallen in the door he had just finished sabotaging her shower to get rid of her, and had assumed that spurious, but oh, so convincing air of concern to distract her. And how well it had worked, she thought wretchedly.

As had his kiss. Guaranteed to keep the little woman from asking any awkward questions.

Without having noticed either the petunias or the geraniums, Nicola found herself on the front step of the house. Because she was too early for breakfast the corridor was deserted, although she caught a tantalising whiff of bacon and coffee from the kitchen. But the light was on in Olivia's office, for Olivia believed that the early bird got the worm, and had landed three rich husbands to prove it. This morning she was arrayed in purple and green, a giant emerald and diamond lizard crawling up the shoulder of her draped silk top; Nicola in her sweatsuit and rain slicker felt instantly dowdy. 'Nicola,' Olivia said cordially. 'Do come in . . . sit down.'

But Nicola remained standing on the other side of the desk. She said with careful restraint, 'Trent, who does not want me living next door to him because I'm inhibiting his love-life, has removed various vital components from my shower so that it no longer works. He thinks this will cause me to move to the attic room in this house. He's wrong. I want the shower repaired today, Olivia, and a lock put on my door.' She added with belated good manners, 'Please.'

Olivia's eyelids, purple shading to green, drooped over her eyes, although not quite quickly enough to hide the laughter in them. 'How naughty of him,' she murmured.

'It's more than naughty, it's outrageous!' Nicola responded heatedly.

'Certainly Jonathan would never do anything like that,' was Olivia's all too apt reply.

But Nicola was not going to be caught by that one. 'Ah...' she said. 'You might be surprised. I rewrote the tea party scene last night, and Jonathan came off rather well.'

'Did he, indeed?' said Olivia. 'I see. All right, Nicola, I'll see what I can do about a plumber. He'll have to come from Corner Brook, so he may not get here today. But I'll do my best, I promise.' She put her head to one side, and the lizard glinted jovially. 'An alternative is to get Trent to fix the shower when he gets back—he's gone to Corner Brook himself to get some supplies; he can't very well work outdoors today because of the rain.'

'No, thanks—he'd probably cut off my entire water supply. A plumber, Olivia, please. And a locksmith.'

'The plumber I can guarantee. But I don't want locks on any of the doors here, Nicola, I feel it's important to the spirit of the place that we trust one another. I'll speak to Trent about the shower. He won't do anything like that again.'

'I'd much rather you didn't. *I* can handle Trent.' And Nicola looked very fierce.

Again amusement flitted across Olivia's face. 'Very well. In the meantime, why don't you use Trent's shower this morning? He's on his way to Corner Brook—you'll be quite safe. But you'd better hurry—omelettes and bacon for breakfast in fifteen minutes.'

So Nicola hurried. Back in her own bathroom she gathered shampoo, soap and towels, then left her side of the cabin and boldly walked up Trent's steps. But on the top step she halted. She might have Olivia's permission, but this still felt very much like trespassing. Gran would not have approved.

Trent had trespassed on her side. Tit for tat.

She knocked on the door, and as she waited for the response that she knew would not come, she heard her pulse throbbing in her ears. Then she pulled the door open.

The living-room was noticably tidier than it had been on the day she had arrived. Two days ago, she thought in surprise. A lot seemed to have happened in two days. She tiptoed across the room, almost as if she expected Trent to burst out of the bedroom and demand an explanation for her presence. The bedroom door was ajar. Pulled by a force she could not have denied, and which was far stronger than mere curiosity, Nicola peered in.

The room was, of course, empty. The bed, a three-quarter size with a plain wooden headboard the mate of her own, stood against the wall. It was neatly made, the white chenille spread without a wrinkle. The built-in cupboard, which like her own, had no door, revealed a tidy row of jeans and shirts on hangers; the top of the dresser held an array of toilet articles, a leather wallet, and a gold watch.

Greatly daring, Nicola stepped into the room, nearer to the dresser. The name on the watch was Piaget. Nicola had never been to New York or London or Paris, but Gayle had had a subscription to *Vanity Fair* and Cheryl to *Vogue*, and Nicola knew such a watch was very expensive. The wallet was leather, the word Gucci inscribed in one corner.

Not the kind of things she would have expected a gardener to own. By now intensely curious, disregarding the fact that she would be late for breakfast, Nicola knelt to investigate the contents of the walnut bookshelf that stood under the window next to a small hotplate and refrigerator, the same as the ones in her living-room. The shelves held the latest John Updike, biographies of Virginia Woolf and Sigmund Freud, a book of statistical analysis for businessmen that, when she flipped it open, looked incredibly complicated, and a very beautiful book of modern European architecture.

There was not one book on gardening. Nor, she thought as she got to her feet, was there a single photograph in the room.

Distantly through the mist the breakfast bell chimed. With a guilty start, wondering how she could have wasted so much time, Nicola hurried to the bathroom. It, too, was very tidy, and smelled pleasantly of aftershave and of the soap hanging on a rope in the shower.

She dumped her belongings on the toilet cistern, stripped off her clothes, and pushed aside the plastic curtain to turn on the shower. A gush of water bounced off the opposite wall of the cubicle. Her eyes stormy, she remembered the four drops of water that had been all she could coax out of her own, and stepped under the hot, stinging spray. It felt wonderful.

She soaped her body and rinsed it, then reached for her shampoo, pouring a small amount into her palm. It always made a copious lather, one of the reasons she liked this brand; rubbing her scalp vigorously, she rather wished she knew some Spanish bar songs, for it was amazing what a lift a little hot water could give to one's spirits. Instead she began singing John Denver's latest hit at the top of her voice.

The cubicle's plastic curtain was ripped aside. Trent said furiously, 'What the hell do you think you——?' His jaw dropped. 'My God, it's you.'

His face was blank with astonishment. Nicola, whose mouth had also fallen open, inhaled a gob of lather and spat it out hastily. More lather slid down the pink-tipped curve of her breast; her skin glowed, sleek and wet, water trickling down her flat belly and slender thighs. She saw his eyes drop, and, with a muffled sound between a groan and a yelp, she seized the curtain from his slack fingers and wrapped as much of herself in it as she could. 'You're in Corner Brook!' she gasped.

A wide smile spread across his face. 'No, Nicola. I'm here. You're getting water all over the floor.'

As she reached for the taps, the curtain fell away from her body. She grabbed it again. 'Turn the taps off, Trent,' she choked. 'Olivia told me you'd gone to Corner Brook for supplies.'

'Quite true. But I was halfway there and realised I'd forgotten my wallet. So I came back to get it. And found you.' He sketched a gallant, if somewhat overdone, bow. 'An unexpected pleasure.'

'The taps, Trent.'

He reached around her and turned the hot and cold taps off simultaneously. Nicola, her face framed in white foam, said trenchantly, 'You thought I was somebody else. Suzie.'

'I did. Suzie is after me, as you may or may not have noticed.'

Momentarily forgetting her naked body and soapy hair, Nicola said, 'I thought it was a mutual pursuit—in fact, you said it was. But you were furious when you pulled the curtain back. When you thought I was Suzie.'

'I am not interested in Suzie,' Trent said flatly. 'Quite apart from any other considerations, I can't stand chipped nail polish.'

Regrettably Nicola laughed, a full-throated, infectious laugh that echoed delightfully in the tiny cubicle. Trent began to laugh as well, his eyes a brilliant blue, a lock of hair falling over his forehead.

Nicola saw this, and was aware of a strong urge to brush it back. She clutched the curtain more tightly, which caused it to plaster itself against her skin; the plastic was neither very thick nor very opaque, and with a gasp of dismay she took a step backwards. 'I'm going to be late for breakfast,' she sputtered, then heard her incorrigible tongue add, 'I thought you spent last night with Suzie.'

'I did not. I got up around six-thirty and went over to the house to fix my own breakfast.'

Knowing she very badly wanted the answer, she said, 'Why did you lie to me about Suzie?'

His face closed. 'Because I didn't want you living next door to me, and I figured if you thought a torrid love-affair was in progress between Suzie and me, you'd leave.'

'You really didn't want me next door, did you?'

'Not just you—anyone,' was the impatient reply.

'You're a loner,' she said thoughtfully.

'Always have been.'

'So why are you now telling me the truth, Trent? About Suzie, I mean.'

'I don't like lying.' He shrugged his shoulders irritably, and she sensed the words were against his own volition. 'Especially to you.'

She hesitated. 'What's so special about me?'

'You might yell a lot, Nicola, but I still get the feeling you're honest. And I do have to admit that life has been considerably more interesting since you arrived.' With an undertone of intense frustration he added, 'I've been going crazy with boredom ever since I got here.'

Nicola said carefully, 'So you don't mind me living here now?'

'I'll put up with it.'

He looked, however, less than pleased at the prospect. Hurt, she said, 'You're a hard man to get to know.'

'You don't have to get to know me. In fact, I don't want you trying.'

His jaw was tight and any memory of laughter had long since vanished from his face. Knowing she was risking another rebuff, Nicola asked, 'Why are you such a loner?'

He was plainly regretting the direction the conversation had taken. 'If we're going to live next door to each other, you've got to stop asking questions,' he said in a clipped voice. 'Is that clear?'

Keep off. That was the message. He had no intention of permitting her to allay the frustration she had glimpsed, whose source she could only guess at. A deep well of frustration, she was sure of that. She remembered the Piaget watch and the Gucci wallet—presumably the wallet that was the reason for his return—and said sharply, 'Trent, you're not a famous author in disguise, are you? Someone I should know?'

Her words had touched a nerve. She suddenly saw quite another man, a dangerous man whose eyes gleamed like the blue blade of a knife and whose muscles had tensed as if he were about to leap on her. Gone was the air of mockery; in its place was a ruthless hunter poised to strike. Wishing her words unsaid, her knuckles white on the edge of the shower curtain, she cried wildly, 'Don't look at me like that!'

He said, his words flailing her defenceless body like hailstones, 'I am not a famous author. Not a writer at all. I'm the gardener, Nicola—the gardener! And my private life, which I live here in this cabin, is strictly my own business. Not yours. Do you understand?'

It would have been all too easy to say, Yes I understand, or, Trent, I'm sorry. All too easy to have shrunk away from him in fear. But last night Olivia had used words like 'prim' and 'proper', and had told Nicola she needed to loosen up; last night it had not been her hero and heroine who were on trial, it had been Nicola. 'No, I don't understand,' she replied with only the slightest of quivers in her voice. 'How could I?'

As Trent took a single step towards her, his foot stubbing against the metal base of the shower cubicle, Nicola did shrink back; she could not have prevented herself. He grated, 'Don't pry into my life—it could get you into trouble. Bad trouble. That's what I'm saying. And you're certainly intelligent enough to grasp that.'

Her breath shuddered in her throat. She retorted with something less than truth, considering the way she had snooped in his bedroom, 'You flatter yourself that I'd be interested enough in your life to bother prying.'

She was shivering with cold. But she had refused to allow her eyes to drop, they were wide with a mixture of defiance and fear. Trent gave an incoherent exclamation, said roughly, 'Finish your shower, for God's sake, before you freeze to death. But remember what I said—keep your nose out of my business.'

He turned on his heel and marched out of the bathroom, closing the door not very gently behind him. Nicola listened, her heart pounding uncomfortably under the clammy curtain, as he went into the bedroom, then crossed the living-room and let the screen bang shut. She waited for two or three minutes, trying to subdue her shivering, until she was sure he had really gone. Then she dropped the curtain, turned the shower on full blast, and rinsed the foam from her hair.

Twelve minutes later Nicola rushed into the dining-room, her hair still damp, her eyes overbright. She had resolutely blanked those last few minutes with Trent out of her mind, for she had no idea what they signified and they had genuinely frightened her; breakfast was what she needed. The remains of the omelette were a little dry, but still edible; after taking generous portions of bacon and toast, and pouring herself a cup of coffee, Nicola sat down beside Harry, a shy middle-aged man who was writing a history of the Portuguese who in the fifteenth century had fished for cod off the coasts of Newfoundland. Harry was not shy at all when coaxed on to his favourite subject. She listened with half an ear to his soft-voiced description of how the cod were preserved for the European markets, and tucked into the omelette.

Nicola was being told rather more than she wanted to know about the ravages of scurvy among the fishermen when Olivia wandered into the room in a flutter of purple and green. Her eyes lit on the couple still at the table. 'There you are, Nicola! The plumber, such a sweet young man, will be here at three o'clock—will you let him in and show him the problem?'

'With pleasure,' said Nicola, seizing the opportunity to escape from Harry's all too graphic descriptions, so graphic that they were making her feel slightly queasy. Nor did the queasiness entirely subside until she was back in her own side of the cabin without sight or sound of Trent and with the door firmly latched behind her. After sorting the pages of her manuscript into order, she began to read, stopping frequently to put notations in the margins.

Two hours later she knew without a doubt that Olivia had been right. The descriptions were good. But her hero was a bore and her heroine deserved him.

She sharpened her pencil and made notes on a pad. She turned on the computer and started with page one, trying to liven up the dialogue, to make Jonathan less stodgy—had George not been the tiniest bit stodgy?—

and more assertive—Allan had not shown much asser-
tiveness, had he? Maryanne, it soon appeared, was quite
prepared to take on a sexier, more ruthless hero. But
Jonathan, with his black hair and his pale grey eyes,
would not co-operate. Jonathan was not particularly sexy
and not even remotely ruthless.

Wrestling with every page, deleting whole paragraphs
at a time, Nicola struggled on. She paced the living-room
floor. She tugged at her hair and chewed the end of her
pencil. She ignored the plangent chiming of the lunch
bell and the screeching of blue jays in the pines, and
nearly jumped off her chair when a loud knock came
on her door and a cheerful voice called, 'Come to fix
the shower, ma'am.'

Hurriedly Nicola pushed the save button. It couldn't
be three o'clock. But her watch said five past three, and
the man on the steps was undoubtedly the plumber.
Rubbing her eyes, which were stinging from scrutinising
the screen so closely, she said, 'Hello. I'm Nicola...come
in.'

He was gangly and red-haired, with ingenuous blue
eyes, and looked as if he should still be tucked behind
a desk in school; he was carrying a red metal tool chest
in one hand and a very large ghetto blaster in the other.
His name, he said, was Charlie. 'What seems to be the
problem?'

Discovering that she was delighted to be interrupted,
for Jonathan had been getting on her nerves, Nicola led
him into the bathroom and turned on the taps. One dispirited drop plopped to the floor of the cubicle.

'Well, now, that is a problem,' said Charlie. 'You leave
it to me. I'll have it working in no time. Although it's
a real old-timer, I'll tell you that—I hope I got parts
that'll fit.'

'There's a similar one next door,' Nicola remarked.

'Maybe I'll take a look at that one first. You mind if I put on a bit of music?'

Charlie's idea of a bit of music was Alice Cooper played at top volume; Nicola retreated to the living-room to tidy her desk. While Charlie bustled back and forth, busy with wrenches and T-bends and whistling cheerfully to himself, she decided to print all her revisions. The noise of the printer would scarcely bother Charlie. Or Alice Cooper. Although, she thought, she was far from satisfied with the changes she had made.

Damn Jonathan! Why wouldn't he come to life? And what did he have to say about her previous ill-starred love-affairs? About George, whom she had adored when she was nineteen, and Allan, with whom she had fallen in love last year at university? Sure, her sisters had whisked them both away. But they, she thought slowly, had allowed themselves to be whisked. Had they, like Jonathan, been something less than real men? Not the right men for her at all?

She had never quite looked at her love-life this way before; it had been easier to blame her sisters. Frowning prodigiously, she hit the two buttons for the print program.

The printer was noisy, and rather slow; wishing she had ear-plugs, Nicola braved the racket in the bathroom to see how Charlie was doing. He had left a ring of greasy fingerprints around the shower head and a great many tools on the floor, but when he turned on the hot tap, water gushed out. 'Just have to tighten things up,' he said, rubbing his hands on a filthy rag. 'Someone's been tampering with it, 's far as I could see.'

'Really?' said Nicola, who knew he was right.

'Yeah...I figure parts from this one ended up next door. You see my big wrench anyplace?'

She could not. 'Must've left it next door—had to take that one apart to check the threads,' he said. 'You want to run and get it while I clean up here?'

'Sure,' said Nicola, and escaped to comparative silence outdoors. However, it was raining harder than it had all day, so she quickly pulled Trent's door open and went inside. The wrench was nowhere to be seen in the bathroom, which Charlie, surprisingly, had left very clean. She did a cursory search of the living-room then headed for the door, deciding he must have mislaid it among all the scattered tools on her bathroom floor. But as she reached for the handle of the screen, her heart missed a beat. Trent had just emerged from the pine trees and was striding across the wet grass. His head was down, his hands thrust in the pockets of his jeans; his face was scored with frustration, and for all his long strides he looked like an animal cooped up in a cage.

Then he looked up and saw her there. He stopped dead. His brows drew together; his lips thinned. Knowing she must look the picture of guilt, Nicola said in a voice that sounded unconvincing even to her, 'I just came to get——'

In one bound he had reached the bottom of the steps, and in another the top. He wrenched the door open, circling her arm with a grip like a manacle and shoving her further into the room. 'What the devil do I have to do to convince you to leave me alone?' he thundered.

'I was looking for——'

'I don't want you here, I don't want you living next door, I wish to God I'd never laid eyes on you. Don't you *ever* come in here again—do you hear me?'

His face was livid, and, even in the midst of a confused mixture of fear and fury, Nicola was aware that he did not look, nor was he behaving, the slightest bit like Jonathan. 'Let go!' she cried.

'Somehow I've got to get it through your thick skull that you don't just wander in and out of here as the mood takes you—weren't you ever taught to respect other people's privacy? I've never met anyone as thick-headed, as rude, as insensitive, as you! And you would have to end up next door to me.'

Not knowing which of his adjectives she hated the most, Nicola kicked out with a sandalled foot. But her big toe connected with the steel tip of Trent's work boot. 'Ouch!' she said, and then the words came tumbling from her tongue. 'It's not me who's rude, Trent Livingstone, it's you. Because I've been trying to tell you why I'm here, and have you listened? Oh, no, you're too busy proving what a macho——'

But he was not listening. A nasty smile on his face, he said, 'A possible motive's just occurred to me…could it be that you, like Suzie, are—shall we say, interested in me? "Pursuit" was the word we used this morning when I found you in my shower, wasn't it? And very charming you looked, too. So what was the next strategy up your sleeve, Nicola—tuck yourself in the bedroom and wait until I came home? Was that the plan?'

Incoherent with rage, Nicola babbled, 'You're the last man I'd ever——' Then she stopped talking for the simple reason that Trent had closed her lips with his own.

Nicola had been kissed before; neither George nor Allan had been quite that backward. It was also the second time Trent had kissed her. But she had never been kissed like this, with such confidence, such unabashed sensuality, such a deliberate assault on her senses. And all the while that his mouth was moving with subtle insistence against hers, Trent's hands were seeking out the curve of her spine, pressing her close to the warmth of his body, the lean length of chest and belly and thigh.

Her anger melted like wax in a candle flame. In a pool of heat Nicola surfaced to desire, a languid desire that bathed her limbs in longing and her heart in the power of passion. She forgot everything: her rage, her reason for being in Trent's cabin, the pounding of rock music through the thin walls with its beat that echoed the throb of blood in her veins. The world both narrowed and expanded; narrowed to the circle of Trent's arms, expanded to a wordless, limitless ache of hunger.

Then Trent raised his head to speak to her. Nicola did not want words; her eyes huge over cheeks flushed a delicate pink, she fought to hear and understand what he was saying.

'So I was right,' he was drawling with lazy assurance. 'I rather suspected the first time I kissed you that you were hiding unexpected talents, Nicola Shea. Good. This summer so far has been a total and unmitigated disaster—I might as well do something to improve it.' He raised one brow. 'Tonight? My place or yours?'

She was staring at him as though he were a member of another species, and although she opened her mouth no sound came out. He said sharply, 'Come on, Nicola, you don't have to play the innocent—why else were you here?'

She croaked, 'You think I came here to—to seduce you.' As he nodded, she gave a crazy cackle of laughter. 'That would be the last thing in the world I'd be likely to do,' she said with absolute and unmistakable truth.

His mouth tightened. 'Come off it—you didn't dislike what we were doing. Don't try and tell me that, because I won't believe you.'

Sluggishly Nicola's brain had begun to function again. 'You've got a lousy opinion of women,' she whispered. 'You don't even know me, and what you do know you don't like. But you'd go to bed with me because you're bored. Because you're having a bad summer.' Anger stirred to life again in her breast. 'You've got the wrong woman, Trent Livingstone. Buy Suzie some new nail polish and take Suzie to bed. Because you're not taking me.'

'No?' he said silkily. 'I could change your mind, I'm sure.'

Remembering that one kiss, Nicola knew he could be right. But he was not going to get the chance to prove it. 'Don't touch me,' she snapped. 'I wouldn't go to bed with you if you were the only man in a thousand miles. I don't like you any more than you like me—how could we possibly make love together?'

With an ugly laugh he said, 'There are shorter words for what we'd do, Nicola.'

She felt cheapened and diminished by his words, as though she would never feel clean again. She also felt very close to tears. 'You're despicable,' she said, and to her horror heard her voice break. 'If you treat everyone like this, I can see why you're a loner—nobody would want to be with you. You certainly don't have to worry that I'll ever come over here again—I won't come within ten feet of you if I can help it.'

As she turned to go, knowing she could not take much more of this, Trent said harshly, 'You're fooling yourself, you know that, don't you? But if you insist on going back to your place, you can turn that goddamned radio off—I can't hear myself think.'

As if on cue the pounding percussion from next door was cut off in mid-bar. Into the echoing silence Charlie called, 'All through, ma'am.'

'Who's that?' Trent rapped.

'The plumber,' Nicola said in a dull voice. 'He came to fix the shower.'

Charlie's head appeared through the screen; the ghetto blaster was tucked under one arm, tenderly wrapped in his jacket. 'You won't have no trouble with the shower now, ma'am,' he said. 'Good as new. I found the wrench, too—hadn't left it over here after all.' With a gap-toothed grin he added, 'I'll send the old lady the bill. Bye for now.'

Olivia would not appreciate being called the old lady, thought Nicola, and reached for the door-handle. Trent said urgently, 'Nicola, wait...I owe you an apology.'

'You owe me several,' she said flatly. 'But I don't want them. You made it abundantly clear what you think of me, and no apology will wipe that out. And the tables have turned, Trent—now I'm asking *you* to stay away from *me*.'

He dropped a hand on her shoulder; its weight and warmth inescapably reminded her of the devastating power of his kiss. Furious with herself for remembering and with him for daring to touch her, she twisted free. As she pushed the door open he said in a voice she might not have recognised as his, 'I misjudged you—I'm truly sorry.'

She made the mistake of looking back. His face was bleak; it was plain he did not expect her to listen to him, equally plain that he had had to say the words. With an incoherent expression of distress, Nicola tumbled down the steps into the rain.

She could not bear to go meekly to her own side of the cabin and listen to the small sounds of him moving around, separated from her by only a wall. So she darted between the wet trees, flinching as a shower of drops trickled down her back, the pine needles springy beneath her feet. There was a library in the house; she would wait there for dinner, and after dinner she would work on chapter three.

The library was on the second floor of the house, next to a small oak-panelled cubicle that housed a pay telephone for the use of the writers. The cubicle was empty, as was the library, an elegant high-ceilinged room that could have graced an English country mansion. Nicola wandered along the shelves, seeing only a pair of bleak blue eyes rather than discerning titles and authors; after picking out a book at random, she curled up in one of the velvet-covered armchairs, staring sightlessly at the cover of the book and wishing she had never come to the Eyrie.

CHAPTER FOUR

NICOLA had no idea how long she had been sitting in the library before she was pulled back to reality by the sound of a voice. An all-too-familiar voice. Trent's. He was talking on the telephone just outside the door, she thought, horrified, and lifted her hands to plug her ears. But then the fury and desperation with which he was speaking stopped her in mid-air.

'You're no nearer an arrest than you were four weeks ago. For God's sake, man, move! I'm going crazy stuck out here in the woods watching the weeds grow.'

Silence, during which Nicola sat as still as a mouse. Then Trent burst out, 'OK, OK, I know you're doing what you can—it's just not enough. I'm not going to give you much longer, Tony. If he hasn't turned up soon, I'm coming back and to hell with the consequences.'

Another charged silence. Trent said furiously, 'No! I don't want to be here. I don't give a damn if it's summer and I need a holiday—I want out.' He added an irritable goodbye and slammed down the receiver with a violence that made Nicola jump. Then she heard him run down the stairs, taking them two at a time. The front door also slammed.

Nicola got up and replaced the book on the shelves, not even noticing its title. She was almost sure Trent had been speaking to the police . . . what was he mixed up in? Where did he want to return to so urgently that he would disregard any consequences? Finally—and painfully—was she the reason he did not want to be here?

* * *

Nicola did not work on chapter three that evening. Harry had sighted a pair of pileated woodpeckers on one of his rambles up the road, and had told Karen, who had never seen one and who commandeered Nicola to go with her to try and find them. Nicola had no idea what a pileated woodpecker looked like, but she did know she had a vast reluctance to see Trent again today, and a hike in the woods would keep her away from the cabin until dark.

Rather to her surprise she enjoyed herself. Karen was a knowledgeable guide, pointing out any number of brightly coloured warblers flitting through the trees, and they did see the woodpeckers, large ungainly black and white birds with brilliant red caps. Afterwards Karen invited her back to her cabin for tea, so the sun had set and the woods were full of shadows when Nicola threaded her way through the pine trees to go to bed. The entire cabin was in darkness. Deeply grateful, she hurried indoors, latched the door and got undressed.

She went to bed feeling heartsore, for she had experienced something new that day: passion in all its power and beauty. But this gift had been thrown back in her face, had been cheapened and degraded. Trent, who had kissed her with such magic, had done so to entice her into his bed. Because he was going crazy stuck in the woods. Because he was bored.

But if she went to bed feeling sorry for herself, Nicola woke to a different emotion altogether. Sunshine was dancing against the window through the trees, which echoed to the harsh calls of the blue jays, and the rooms next door were quiet; outwardly there was nothing to account for the way she felt. For she had woken to anger. Anger blazing red within her, warming all her limbs. Anger that filled her with energy and made her leap out of bed, her feet hitting the floor with a thud. She knew exactly what she was going to do about Trent Livingstone.

In the shower, scarcely noticing the sting of hot water against her body, she let her plan circle in her mind. First she was going to get rid of Jonathan, whom she thoroughly disliked. He was boring and ineffective and dull. No heroine in her right mind would think of getting into bed with him, let alone marrying him. Imagine a lifetime of waking in the morning to find Jonathan's head on the pillow beside yours! No, Jonathan had to go. And in his place she would have a new hero. A man with ruthless blue eyes that could cut like a knife blade through all Maryanne's defences, and a baritone voice that could caress like velvet or roar like thunder. A man who would kiss a woman until she melted in his arms, and then thrust her away with arrogant disregard for her feelings. A man like Trent.

His name, Nicola thought, towelling herself so energetically that her skin glowed, would be Flint. Because that was what he was like. Hard as stone, yet sparks flying whenever he was near.

No more Jonathans. No more men who were putty in the hands of women like her sisters. Flint would call the shots. Flint would do exactly as he pleased, and his trail would be marked by the broken hearts of the women he had known and cast aside. For along with ruthlessness and arrogance and inscrutable blue eyes, Flint was also sexy. Incredibly and irresistibly sexy.

That would be her revenge on Trent for the way he had treated her, Nicola thought as she jogged through the pines to the house for breakfast. She would put him in her book. She would study him as if he were an insect on a pin; she would treat him as the object he had made of her.

He would become—oh, delicious irony—her hero.

When she entered the dining-room a couple of minutes later she saw him immediately. He was sitting by himself at the far end of the table, isolated from everyone else in a way that became explicable as soon as she walked in the door. For he had been watching for her; he signalled to her, pushed back his chair and crossed the room towards her.

She waited calmly, a brilliant smile on her lips, and before he could speak said cordially, 'Good morning, Trent.'

A flicker of uncertainty, of surprise, crossed his features. However, he said with equal cordiality, 'Hello, Nicola...will you join me for breakfast?'

'I'd like that—save me a place.' She produced another brilliant smile, and wondered with faint amazement if she had missed her calling; perhaps she should have been an actress. Because she did not feel at all cordial. As he smiled back at her, she remembered how his lips had imprinted themselves on hers and gave an inward shudder. Yesterday afternoon, fuelled by anger and discontent, he had deliberately set out to seduce her, and she was almost sure that had he been only slightly more circumspect about his motives, and had Charlie the plumber not infringed on the scene, he would have succeeded. She would have fallen, dazzled, into his arms, like the innocent virgin she was. And then she would have found out how she had been used.

As she helped herself to cereal, fruit and coffee, Nicola held an entirely coherent conversation with Karen about the prospects of a game of tennis that afternoon, and then headed towards the end of the table. Trent was still sitting by himself. He had pulled out the chair across from him. Nicola sat down, stirred her coffee, and said demurely, 'You were very quiet getting up this morning, Trent—I didn't hear a sound.'

'I didn't intend that you should.'

'So you're a reformed character?' she said lightly, studying him through her lashes. His blue eyes were unquestionably inscrutable, and his jaw taut. She avoided his mouth, and concentrated instead on the gleam of light in his thick, streaked hair; tawny would be a good way to describe it, she thought. Tawny as a lion's mane. Rather enjoying herself, she began to eat her cereal, which she had mixed with fruit.

Trent said roughly, 'You look very pleased with yourself this morning.'

'A good night's sleep always does wonders for me...this is wonderful melon, isn't it? Or didn't you have any?'

'I didn't ask you to join me to talk about melon, Nicola.' He leaned forwards, resting his forearms on the table, his eyes fastened on her face. 'I want to say again how sorry I am for the way I behaved yesterday.'

He had clasped his hands together. Fascinated by the play of muscles under the tanned skin, Nicola said absently, 'Oh, that's all right.' He was not wearing the Piaget watch, although there was a band of white skin around his left wrist; those hands, she thought with unwilling truth, had held her, waist and hip, against his body in an embrace that even now suffused her with remembered heat.

'That's not what you were saying yesterday.'

She glanced up. 'Sorry?' she said.

'Nicola, would you please listen to me?' he exploded.

His eyes were no longer inscrutable; their expression hovered between—she sought for accuracy—exasperation and anger. 'I'm listening,' she said politely.

He ran his fingers through his hair. 'Then why do I feel as though you're a million miles away?'

His hair—thick, soft, very clean—fell back into place. Nicola took a sip of coffee. 'I'm not. As you can see. Although I seem to recall that yesterday you would have liked me to be.'

'I was in a foul mood all day yesterday. So I took it out on you.' He hesitated, then plunged on. 'I knew when I accused you of—well, there's no really polite way to say it, is there? Of putting the make on me—that I was wrong. That you wouldn't behave that way. But something drove me to say it.' Moving his shoulders restlessly beneath his thin shirt, a movement that intrigued her, he finished, 'I'm truly sorry—please believe me.'

Would Flint apologise with such undoubted sincerity? Or would he seize her in his arms, bend her back across the table and ravish her mouth with kisses, with magnificent disregard for all the other occupants of the dining-room?

Nicola's eyes suddenly widened as she realised where her thoughts had carried her. Flint wouldn't kiss *her*, Nicola. He'd be kissing Maryanne.

Unnerved by her slip, she took a big mouthful of cereal and fruit and mumbled, 'It's OK.'

Trent's voice sharpened. 'Are you sure you're all right? You look as though you're only half here.'

If he got too suspicious he wouldn't spend any more time with her. Nicola swallowed, smiled with as much sincerity as she could muster, and said with a complete disregard for truth, 'You're forgiven.'

'That's better.' And suddenly he smiled back, a smile of such real pleasure that she felt ashamed of herself; it was also an extremely attractive smile that mingled her shame with a mixture of other emotions she did not particularly want to examine.

Attractive was too weak a word. Charged with masculine energy? Magnetic?

Magnetic, Nicola thought, and fought against the pull. She said with admirable casualness, 'I'm glad that's straightened out, then. If we're to live next door, there's no point in us being enemies.'

He said slowly, 'That's not what you were saying yesterday. What changed you, Nicola?'

She addressed herself to her cereal again, casting about for a reason that would convince him. 'Oh, one of my grandmother's sayings was that you shouldn't let the sun go down on your anger...I was brought up by my grandmother.'

'Were you? So was I.'

Caught by the tension in Trent's voice, Flint temporarily forgotten, Nicola glanced up. She said carefully, 'You don't look as though it was a very happy experience...wasn't she good to you?'

'No.'

It was astonishing how a single monosyllabic response could express so much. Don't ask questions. Keep your distance. Stay away. Disregarding all of them, Nicola asked, 'How old were you when you went to live with her?'

'Four.'

'You're sure an expert on the short answer,' she said, exasperated.

'Yeah...' With obvious reluctance he asked, 'How old were you?'

'I was seven.' For a moment the shadow of all the old nightmares flitted across her face, her eyes deep pools of pain.

'So we each have our dark places,' Trent said shrewdly. 'And each of us is alone in them.'

Feeling her way, Nicola said, 'Maybe if we shared them, they'd disappear. And the nightmares would become...just a dream.'

'I've never learned to share. And I'm too old to start now.'

'The loner.'

'Right.' For a moment his hands tensed on the table. 'Do you want to go for a row on the bay this afternoon?'

She gulped, unwittingly his invitation had touched on one of her greatest vulnerabilities. 'I can't—I'm playing tennis with Karen.'

'It's supposed to be the hottest day so far this summer...maybe after supper?'

Torn, because she could not possibly go out in a boat yet she wanted every opportunity to observe him, she said, 'Maybe we could go for a walk—I want to work some of the evening.'

'You'd be safer in a boat.' Little devils of mischief danced in his eyes. 'I can't possibly seduce you in the bottom of a dory.'

'You're not going to try,' Nicola retorted in a flash. 'You apologised for that.'

'I apologised for the way I addressed the issue. I did not say I didn't want to seduce you.'

She sat up straight in her chair. 'Stop it, Trent,' she said in a furious whisper. 'Stop pretending.'

'Pretending?' he repeated blankly. 'Oh, there's no pretence.'

'Of course there is!' she hissed. 'Men want to seduce women like Suzie. Not someone like me.'

'And just how would you describe someone like you, Nicola?' he asked, a peculiar note in his voice.

It was the same question Olivia had asked her. 'I'm not sexy like Suzie. I'm just ordinary.'

To her utter surprise he threw back his head and laughed, a laugh of such real amusement that both Karen and Rafe glanced down the table at them and smiled in

sympathy. Nicola snapped, 'Behave yourself—everyone's looking at us.'

'I promise I won't share the joke.'

'This isn't funny!'

'You're forgetting something.' As he leaned forwards
again, Nicola fought a crazy urge to abandon her
breakfast and run from the room. 'You're forgetting that
I saw you in the shower.' His voice roughened. 'Your
body is exquisite. And your eyes—they're beautiful, too.
Let me tell you something about myself, Nicola. When
I was a kid—oh, five or six—I used to spend a lot of
time in the woods behind my grandmother's house. By
myself. It was low ground, very wet, and I'd come across
these small woodland pools, dark brown peaty water,
clear yet full of mysterious depths, and I'd sit there for
hours staring into the water trying to figure things out.'
Abruptly he straightened, as though already regretting
his confidences. 'Your eyes are like those pools. A man
could lose himself in them . . .'

Neither George nor Allan had ever said anything remotely like this to her. Nicola gazed across the table,
dumbfounded.

'For God's sake!' Trent muttered. 'You look as though
no one's ever complimented you before.'

Driven to truth, she croaked, 'Not like that.'

'And before you accuse me of any ulterior motives,
my motives are, at this particular moment, pure. I have
no intention of seducing you on the dining-room table
in front of a crowd of writers. Some of whom would
probably take notes.'

Trent. Flint. Take notes. Nicola gaped at him and felt
colour creep up her cheeks. 'You're impossible!' she
exclaimed.

'You blush quite charmingly,' he replied, picking up
his mug and plate and pushing away from the table.

'Also, I find I'm beginning to like you—quite a lot. I'll check with you at dinner whether you want to go out in the dory. Good luck with the book.'

Nicola, left alone with her cereal, took another mouthful. He could not possibly have guessed that she intended to model her new hero on him. He couldn't read her mind. She was quite safe.

Safe, but ashamed, she thought honestly. His straightforward apology had impressed her, and when he had said he liked her she had felt an emotion she could only call pleasure. Her motive of revenge was beginning to seem more tawdry the more Trent became a real person to her: a man who had known unhappiness, a man who desired her.

She finished her breakfast, went back to the cabin and turned the computer on. After creating a new directory and file, for this was to be a very different book, she made herself put Trent's image firmly in front of her and began to type. The work went slowly, for she was feeling her way; but the first scene between Maryanne and Flint crackled with so much energy that the pale ghost of Jonathan fled through the window.

By lunchtime Nicola had seven pages, and knew they were better than anything she had written so far. She left the cabin, for she was both hungry and tired, and set off through the pine trees. The air was hot and very still, redolent with the tang of sap. She could have a scene in a pine grove, she thought, smoothing the needles between her fingers. A moonlight scene...

Her reverie was interrupted by the rhythmic crack of an axe hitting wood. On impulse she left the trail, ducking under the trees, the noise growing louder; she knew in her bones that the man wielding the axe was Trent and knew, too, that she was intensely curious to see him in his role as gardener. Then, through a screen of pine needles she caught sight of him, and crept closer, parting two boughs to get a better view.

His back was to her, his shirt hanging over the branch of a nearby maple. He had tossed the axe to the ground and was now swinging a pick at the base of a straggly cedar shrub. Although he was shaded by the canopy of trees, his back was slick with sweat and she could hear him grunting with effort.

He had used the word 'exquisite' to her; she could only call beautiful the smooth play of muscle under the tanned skin, the strength implicit in every stroke, the arc of his back and the taut length of his thigh. As though pulled by a magnet, she slipped between the trees and stepped into the open. 'You've chosen a hot day to do that,' she said.

Trent's head jerked up and slowly he straightened. 'Nicola,' he said, and wiped the beads of moisture from his forehead with the back of one hand.

A tangle of blond hair ran from chest to navel; his muscles, compact under the smooth skin, were also beaded with sweat. Very impressive muscles, thought Nicola with unwilling admiration, wondering why on earth she had shown herself. 'What are you doing?' she said inanely.

'Olivia has decided that all these cedars remind her too strongly of mortality.' He grinned. 'So out they come.'

His smile was so irresistible that she found herself smiling back. 'You look different,' she said. 'More relaxed.'

'Nothing like a pickaxe for getting rid of a few frustrations,' he replied lightly. 'You could pass me the shovel if you like.'

She rested her clear brown eyes on his face and said, 'You don't like being here, do you? At the Eyrie, I mean.'

'I could think of other places I'd rather be. Don't pry, Nicola.'

She said conversationally, 'When I was a little girl my parents took me to a zoo. Only once, because I hated it. All those animals in cages and us looking in. The big sad eyes of the bears...I've never forgotten them. There was one bear crouched in the corner of the cage, and if any of the others got too close, he'd growl. That's what you're like, Trent. This place is a cage to you, isn't it?'

'You see far too much,' he said wryly. 'Pass the shovel.'

She grinned at him, a gamine grin full of mischief. 'You invented the word loner,' she teased. 'I'm sure having me next door all summer will be a salutary experience for you.'

'That's one word for it, I suppose. The shovel, Nicola.'

The shovel was leaning against the trunk of the pine nearest her. Nicola picked it up and walked across the narrow strip of grass towards him. Keeping a careful distance away from him, she passed it to him.

Quite deliberately he trapped her fingers in his, his eyes trained on her face. To the shimmer of heat and the scent of pines was added a more homely odour, that of a man's sweat. It was more intimate than Nicola could bear; and she was far too close to the neatly banded muscles of his belly and the rough-haired chest. She gave an involuntary tug of her hand and said breathlessly, 'Don't, Trent.'

He released her immediately. 'Thanks,' he said.

He was thanking her for more than the shovel; her reaction had pleased him, she knew, and cursed herself for having so easily given herself away. Her eyes dropped from his, and for the first time she noticed an angry scar furrowing the muscle at the top of his left arm. A long straight scar, scarcely healed. 'What's that?' she said.

After the briefest of pauses Trent answered, 'A rope burn. I do some rock-climbing.'

George had been an avid fan of spy movies, so Nicola had seen more than her share of them. She remembered the phone call she had overheard and said, 'It looks like a bullet wound to me.'

'All you writers have such vivid imaginations.'

Nonplussed, she gazed up at him. 'What else do you do, besides gardening?'

'Fend off inquisitive females?'

She compressed her lips. 'You have a smart answer for everything, don't you? A smart answer that gives absolutely nothing away.'

'Years of practice,' he said agreeably, 'My turn to ask a question. This is a very hot day. You are wearing cotton trousers. Loose trousers. Baggy trousers. Trousers that don't even hint at the very nice curves I know are underneath. When am I going to see you in shorts, Nicola?'

With a wicked gleam in her eye, she said, 'I have a theory—that the deferral of gratification increases anticipation.'

'I am, right now, the living proof of your theory.'

She had not expected so quick a response. 'The lunch bell rang ten minutes ago,' she said weakly. 'We'll be late.'

'Too much anticipation might cause loss of control...had you thought of that?'

'Since boredom caused you to lose control last time, I'm not overly impressed,' she replied sweetly. 'See you later, Trent.'

She heard him give a soft laugh as she scurried off past the doomed cedars. She had won that round, she thought. Nevertheless, she had definitely better leave any moonlit scenes in the pine grove to the realm of her computer and her imagination. With Trent, in the flesh, she could easily lose control of the plot.

CHAPTER FIVE

AFTER·lunch, where she sat between Rafe and Harry and ignored Trent altogether, Nicola hurried back to the cabin. It was not particularly well insulated, she soon discovered, and by mid-afternoon had become oppressively hot. But Flint and Maryanne, perhaps fuelled by Nicola's encounter with Trent, were behaving exactly as she wanted them to, and she pressed on, knowing with a twinge of malice that Olivia would react very differently to this version. At four o'clock Karen called for her to play tennis; Karen was made of stern stuff and was not to be discouraged by a temperature in the high eighties. 'There's a breeze from the bay,' she said. 'Come on, Nicola, you can't work all the time, it's bad for you. You can work after supper, when it's cooler.'

So Nicola put on shorts and, inspired by Karen's competitiveness, played several very hard games. They were tied in the final game of the last set; Nicola made two inspired serves and an amazing backhand save and won the whole match. Karen hugged her, laughing off her chagrin, and from the sidelines Nicola became aware of the sound of clapping.

She looked over. Trent, shovel leaning against his chest, was responsible for the applause. Karen said, 'Go on over—I'll pick up the balls.'

'Oh, no, I'll help.'

Karen rolled her eyes. 'If I weren't safely married and Trent was clapping for me, I'd be over there like greased lightning. Go, Nicola!'

74

'I pity your husband if you boss him around like this,' Nicola grumbled, and went.

Trent gave her a comprehensive survey from her scarlet face to the toes of her white sneakers. 'Anticipation is fully satisfied,' he remarked. 'You play hard, Nicola.'

'To win,' she said, and with a small shock of surprise knew the words for the truth. She had looked after her grandmother for the eight months it had taken Gran to die of cancer, and had won an acknowledgement of love from that most withholding of women; she had topped her classes at Memorial; when the money from Gran's small inheritance had run out, she had applied to Olivia's writers colony and had been accepted. The only area where she had lost consistently was with men, Nicola thought, frowning at Trent's shirtfront.

'So do I,' said Trent.

Nicola transferred the frown to his face. 'Then why are you hacking down cedar shrubs at the whim of an eccentric old lady?' she demanded, and knew as soon as she had spoken that the question had hit home.

Ice filmed the blue of his eyes. 'How many times do I have to tell you to mind your own business?'

She tilted her chin. 'Game, set and match to me,' she said.

'There'll be other games, Nicola—and don't count on winning them all.' With a curt nod, he wheeled and strode away.

Nicola watched him go. The nice young woman whom Gran had raised seemed to disappear altogether around Trent. She was not normally overly inquisitive about the lives of others; live and let live had been very much her motto. What was it about Trent that caused her to behave so differently?

Then Karen came trotting up behind her. 'You sure got rid of him in a hurry,' she observed. 'He's sort of larger than life, isn't he? My theory is that he's Olivia's illegitimate son—why else would he be buried in a place like this cutting the grass?'

'Grandson, maybe,' Nicola replied, then could have bitten off her tongue. There had been a lot of emotion in Trent's brief mention of his grandmother, and for her to share this information seemed less than honourable. 'Forget I said that,' she added hurriedly. 'I've got to have a shower, Karen; I wouldn't want anyone to get downwind of me right now. See you at dinner...and thanks for the games.'

'I'll be out for blood next time,' Karen said amiably. 'See you tonight at the lobster boil, too.'

'Lobster boil?' Nicola repeated, puzzled.

'Didn't Rafe mention it to you? Every Saturday, weather permitting, we get together on the beach, make a fire, sing, have a few beers. Harry got some lobster from one of his fishing pals, so don't eat too much supper...things usually get under way around nine. Down on the beach near the wharf.'

So at nine-thirty that evening Nicola set out from the cabin to the beach. She had almost decided not to go, because she had worked after dinner as a way of avoiding Trent and the dory, and she was tired; but the evening was warm and the stars close in the sky and she liked the thought of listening to the waves ripple on the beach. So she trudged towards the shore, following the snatches of laughter and song that drifted through the woods.

When she emerged from the trees, she stopped for a minute, the scene etched in her mind. Flames from a huge bonfire leaped and curveted into the sky, sparks trailing streamers of fire like bright orange ribbons. There must have been twenty people gathered around the fire, people Nicola had eaten with and talked to in the dining-room, yet the dancing flames made strangers of them. The faces clustered round the blaze could have been taking part in some ancient ritual, encircled by the vast and impenetrable blackness of the night with only the fire to keep fear at bay. And she, Nicola, the outsider, was the one who stood alone in the darkness...

She gave herself a shake; her imagination was working overtime. Feet crunching in the tiny rounded pebbles of the beach, she began walking towards the fire, and heard Rafe call, a little drunkenly, 'Here's Nicola! Grab yourself a beer, Nicola—lots more where that one came from.'

Karen passed her an open bottle of beer, Harry passed a packet of nachos, and suddenly she was part of the group and no longer the watcher from the darkness. They were all there: Greta, Mickie, Daniel, Elizabeth, Donald...the names ran through her head. As Carmella started singing 'The Wind beneath my Wings', Nicola took a gulp of beer and joined in, the heat of the fire burning through her jeans and searing her cheek. From within the circle of flames the darkness was not nearly so threatening, and the darting reflections of the flames on the shiny black surface of the water were extremely beautiful. She was glad she had come.

Ten minutes later Tad arrived with a guitar, and as empty beer bottles accumulated in the cartons, the singing and the laughter gained volume. Even Harry, tending the lobsters on a Coleman stove to one side, added his voice, a surprisingly robust bass. Then, like an apparition from the night, Suzie appeared, clad in a swirling purple skirt threaded with gilt and a black blouse, her long hair held back by a scarlet scarf. Her bare feet finding confident purchase on the shifting stones, she began to dance, a sinuous gypsy dance that teased and mocked, offering infinite promises only to snatch them away before fruition. Tad, his thin, sensitive face frowning in concentration, picked up the rhythm of the dance with his guitar.

Nicola watched, fascinated, caught in the spell Suzie was weaving, a spell fashioned from both the light and the darkness. But then Rafe, sitting beside her, dropped his beer bottle, and the sharp ring of glass on stone broke the spell for Nicola; his bearded face was acutely unhappy, for Rafe, she knew, had tasted of Suzie's promise and had suffered when it was withdrawn. Nicola passed him a fresh beer, patting his sleeve with mute sympathy, and saw from the corner of her eye another figure emerge from the darkness. Trent.

She was sure it was coincidence that he had arrived so soon after Suzie. Yet even to think of them together in the warm, scented shadows of the forest stabbed Nicola with an emotion she knew was jealousy. It was the intensity of that emotion that frightened her.

Then Suzie began to dance towards Trent, her arms all graceful flowing movement, her head thrown back to bare her throat, her bosom outthrust. She circled him slowly, hips swaying in blatant invitation, a pagan figure in the firelight.

No man could resist that, thought Nicola, and heard the last remnants of the singing falter to silence. Tension screamed along her nerves. Like a wolf on a lonely hilltop, she wanted to lift her face to the sky and howl her misery to the cold, indifferent stars.

In a flourish of barbaric chords Tad ended his accompaniment, and Suzie sank to the ground in front of Trent in a deep, mocking curtsy. Trent bowed elaborately, throwing the mockery back in her face, and said plaintively, 'Isn't anyone going to offer me a beer?'

In a burst of laughter the tension eased. Rafe staggered to his feet and grabbed a bottle from the cooler, Tad played the opening bars of an energetic

Newfoundland jig and Harry called, 'Five minutes and we eat!' Only Nicola was watching Suzie, whose skirt was spread over the stones like the petals of a flower. Suzie pulled a face at Trent's retreating back, got to her feet with lithe grace and set off across the beach to sit by Daniel. Slowly Nicola relaxed the tightness in her shoulders.

Trent sat down by Rafe, tipping his head back to take a deep draught of the beer, the muscles moving in his throat as he swallowed. Then he looked over at Nicola, on the other side of Rafe, and smiled.

His eyes were smiling as well as his mouth; tiny flames were reflected in his irises, and Nicola felt enveloped and held in warmth. Involuntarily she smiled back, shadows moving over her cheekbones and the soft curve of her lips. Rafe hiccupped and said with the seriousness of a man who has drunk too much, 'You watch out for S-Suzie, Trent, old man...she doesn't give a damn for anyone exshept hershelf.' He nodded to himself, as though he had just pronounced a profound truth.

Trent replied just as seriously, 'I will, Rafe—thanks.' But then, as Rafe fumbled with the cap of his next beer, Trent rather spoiled the effect by winking at Nicola.

She felt light-headed, her heart racing in her breast, for the spell he cast was far more potent than Suzie's. And was he not telling her, once again, that he did not care one whit for Suzie?

Yet why was he bothering with her, Nicola? Was he casting his spell as deliberately as Suzie had? And for the same ends?

The scar on his arm was hidden now by his shirt. But Trent was a man hiding far more than a mysterious scar, a scar she was quite sure had nothing whatever to do with rock-climbing. Suddenly afraid, Nicola scrambled to her feet and said breathlessly, 'I'm going to check on the lobster.'

Trent raised a quizzical brow, as though he had both seen and understood her confusion. She scurried across the loose pebbles—how had Suzie danced with such grace on them?—and peered into the huge pot of boiling water on the stove, where she could see the orange bodies of the lobsters bobbing through the steam. Harry had had his share of beer as well; he said with none of his habitual shyness, 'I guarantee you'll never have tasted anything as good as these in your entire life.' He broke off to yell, 'Hey, Trent, come and help me dump the water off, will you?'

Lobsters and water ended up on the sea-scoured pebbles. 'Two each,' Harry announced. 'Melted butter and garlic bread by the fire. Come and eat!'

An assortment of tools was produced to crack the lobster shells, and five minutes later Nicola was seated cross-legged on the beach between Rafe and Trent, munching on garlic bread and the succulent flesh of a claw. Butter dribbled down her chin; she wiped it with the back of her hand, for no one seemed to have thought of napkins, and said contentedly, 'This is as close to heaven as one can get.'

His face full of laughter, Trent leaned over, said in a voice pitched for her ears alone, 'There are other routes to heaven, Nicola,' and with one finger caught a smear of lobster from the corner of her mouth. His touch lingered a moment longer than was necessary, caressing the softness of her lower lip; his meaning was clear.

Caught unawares, Nicola blushed, a slow, creeping heat that crept from her cheeks to her forehead. The brief pressure of his finger had enveloped her in a heat that had nothing to do with the fire; she had never, she thought blankly, felt anything as instant or as fierce with either George or Allan. Yet she had loved George and Allan and she did not love Trent. Was not always sure she liked him, and was less sure she trusted him.

She said, with an attempt at flippancy that did not quite come off, 'I'll stick with lobster, thank you.'

'You can't get away with that, not with me. I watched you play tennis this afternoon—you don't play a safe game at all. And at the end, when the whole match was up for grabs, you took even more risks.' With a snap of his wrists he cracked a tail open from end to end. 'You can learn a lot about people by watching the way they play games.'

She did not like to think of him psychoanalysing her while she dashed around the court oblivious to his presence. 'I can choose which risks to take,' she replied, an edge to her voice.

'I have the feeling there are some you're assiduously avoiding.'

The noise level was fairly high, and no one else appeared to be paying them any attention; not even Suzie, who was now busily batting her lashes at Tad. Nicola said bluntly, 'Sex, you mean.'

Apparently absorbed in extracting the long black thread of the digestive tract from the lobster tail, Trent said absently, 'Wonderful how fast you catch on.'

He was playing with her like a fish on a hook. 'Cut it out, Trent!' she snapped.

There was an odd gentleness in his next question. 'Did some guy pull a dirty on you, Nicola?'

'That's no more your business than the scar on your arm is mine!'

'So he did, and you've been running scared ever since.'

'Oh, it wasn't just one, it was two,' she retorted. 'I don't give up that easily.'

'And I suppose if I say I think they were crazy, you'll laugh in my face.'

She thought of her sisters, her beautiful, confident, sensual sisters, and said in a low voice, 'Yes, I will.'

'You're better off without them,' he said. 'Here, let me crack that for you. But I would suspect you're not ready to admit that yet.' He passed back the claw he had snapped, and added, 'pass me another piece of bread, would you?'

She ripped a chunk of bread from the loaf and handed it to him. 'You seem to think you can dissect my love-life as easily as you can dissect a lobster,' she said irritably. 'Stick to pulling claws apart, Trent—at least that's useful.'

'Oh, the other might be useful too. For you, I mean.' He gave her a sideways grin. 'Who knows, I might benefit as well.'

'If you think I'm going to fall into bed with you just because you're having a boring summer, you can think again! Because——'

'I'm sorry I ever said that,' he interrupted impatiently.

'It was the truth.'

'It was the truth then.'

'So what's changed?'

'I want you for yourself,' he said, so quietly she had to strain to hear the words under the laughter and singing and the crackle of the fire.

It was not the answer she had expected; she remembered how Suzie had danced with such provocative sensuality in front of Trent, and remembered too how the men she had wanted had left her for her sisters. 'I don't believe you!' she said sharply.

'As far as your sexuality is concerned, you've got a classic case of inferiority complex, Nicola Shea.'

Trent had raised his voice; from the corner of her eye Nicola saw Rafe give them a curious glance. Knowing Trent had hit home, hating him for doing so, she said brusquely, 'I see no reason to discuss that with you. Now or ever. Is that clear?'

Trent's eyes lifted to show her the anger she seemed to evoke in him so easily. 'It sure is,' he said. 'After that nice little vote of no-confidence, I think I'll have another beer.' He got to his feet in a single agile movement. 'Excuse me.'

Nicola watched him thread his way to the cooler, take out a beer, and then say something to Greta and Mickie that made them both laugh. He would not be back to sit at her side, she was sure of that. She had driven him away. Because he frightened her? Because he evoked emotions she had not known existed?

Karen sat down beside her, and as if she had read Nicola's mind said, 'You do keep pushing that man away, don't you?'

'He's far too sure of himself...wasn't the lobster great?'

Karen chuckled. 'I can take a hint. This is fun, isn't it?'

Tad was strumming his guitar again, a soft background as Rafe, whom the food appeared to have sobered somewhat, told a wonderfully bizarre ghost story. Karen followed suit with a tale about a great-uncle who had been on the whaling ships. Greta sang a folk song from her native Norway, and, after the group had joined in the choruses, Tad started them on some Newfoundland songs. Nicola sang lustily, trying not to notice how thoroughly Trent was ignoring her. He was ignoring Suzie just as thoroughly, which did not bring her any comfort at all.

Gradually the party wound down. Harry, who liked order, threw the lobster shells into a rubbish bag, and made a neat stack of beer cartons by the cooler; the fire had subsided to a bed of intensely hot coals. Rafe stumbled to his feet to get some water to douse it, and said in sudden inspiration, 'Hey, Nicola's new here—she's never been screeched in!'

'We have no Screech,' said Greta, the practical one. 'Nor a codfish.'

Nicola knew exactly what they were talking about, for it was a tradition for visitors to Newfoundland to down a shot of Screech, a fiery Newfoundland rum, and to kiss a dead codfish. Amused, she said, 'No need—I was born and raised in St John's on the other side of the island.'

But Rafe was not to be deterred. 'Then we'll just do the last bit,' he said. 'C'mon, Tad, Daniel—we've got to have Nicola a true member of the Eyrie.' He kicked at the fire and a shower of sparks shot up into the night; in the glow his bearded face looked demonic.

Still amused, Nicola waited for whatever was going to happen next. Tad leaned his guitar carefully against a piece of grey driftwood and in a burst of energy leaped across the dying fire to land at Nicola's side. Daniel, who looked like a prize fighter without an imaginative bone in his body, yet who wrote plays of haunting desperation, seized Nicola by the arm and pulled her to her feet.

She could not possibly have resisted because he was far too strong. She said with rather overdone pathos, 'Just don't make me chug-a-lug six beers in a row.'

Rafe had stepped out of his deck shoes, pushing them away from the fire. 'Nothing like that,' he said. 'Let's go, guys!'

Quite suddenly Nicola found herself lifted from the ground, Daniel grasping her under the arms, Tad clutching her waist and Rafe her knees. 'Hey,' she said comically, 'what's up? Don't you dump me on the stones, that'd hurt.'

'Got her, Daniel?' Rafe asked rhetorically. 'OK—one, two, three and away we go!'

Their feet skidding on the loose pebbles, they lurched down the slope towards the smooth black water, and Nicola, belatedly realising where they were going, yelped, 'Put me down!'

'You've got to be dunked to belong to the Eyrie,' Tad gasped, wincing as his feet touched the water. 'God, it's cold—you sure this is a good idea?'

Rafe, hauling on Nicola's knees, appeared to have reverted to the level of an adolescent. 'Chicken, Tad?' he taunted, wading deeper into the bay and pulling the others with him.

Nicola fought for calm. 'Listen, Tad,' she said, 'I'm terrified of the water—just drop me here and I'll be OK. But don't go any further. Please.'

There was real urgency in her voice. Tad said, letting go of her so that her body sagged like a sack of grain, 'Sure, this'll do. Let go, Rafe.'

But Rafe was drunk now with more than beer. 'No way,' he cried. 'It's got to be deeper or it won't take. C'mon Daniel.'

'Please put me down,' Nicola repeated, keeping her voice steady with an immense effort.

But the two men surged forward so that the ice-cold water of the bay licked at her back. The water was the stuff of a thousand nightmares, and the precarious calm Nicola had been fighting to preserve deserted her. She shrieked in fear, kicked out with all her strength and felt

Rafe stagger. 'Let me go!' she cried. 'Stop it, Rafe—I tell you, I'm terrified of water!'

But Rafe tightened his grip and yanked on her legs; the beach fell off quite sharply so that he was already chest-deep, grimly fighting to hold on to her. As Daniel gave a shove from behind, Nicola felt the water slosh around her waist and suck noisily at her shoulders. She struggled frantically, thrusting herself backwards against Daniel's chest with all her strength so that he staggered sideways. Water washed over her face, plastering her hair to her scalp, blinding her.

Nicola went berserk. Flailing out with her arms, she struck Daniel hard across the face and lashed out with her feet. Grunting in mingled surprise and pain, Daniel loosened his grip just as she inadvertently caught Rafe across the throat. Rafe let go and Daniel lost his balance.

With a scream of pure terror that was cut off in the middle, Nicola sank beneath the surface. Her mouth and nostrils filled with water. Water pressed in on her on all sides, blinding her; a bottomless, mindless panic devoured her. She was lost. She was going to die, just as her parents had died so many years ago...

From a long way away she felt something seize her by the shoulders. With the last of her energy she fought against it, for what could it be but some nightmare creature of the ocean's depths?

Or Rafe wanting to pull her deeper into the sea.

Whoever or whatever it was, it did not let go. With terrifying strength, a strength far beyond Rafe's, it tugged her through the water. And then suddenly air struck Nicola's face and she drew a choking, agonised breath.

It must be Daniel who was holding her, she thought in renewed terror, and he would do it again, drop her into the sea and leave her to drown; she pounded at his chest with her fists, her body twisting and writhing with frenetic energy. The arms that were holding her tightened their grip. A voice spoke, a deep male voice repeating the same words over and over again in an effort to calm her. But Nicola could not hear the words, for now she was drowning in fear where earlier she had drowned in water, and she was far beyond the reach of reason.

From nowhere a hand struck her cheek. Struck it hard enough so that pain, sharp and shocking, penetrated fear, splitting it open and giving her back the clarity of vision. She was clear of the water. She was being held by a man. But the man was not Daniel. He was Trent.

As he waded up the sloping beach, through harsh rasping breaths that she realised were her own Nicola heard the crunch of pebbles replace the gurgle and slurp of water, and heard, too, Rafe and Daniel mouthing incoherent apologies. In a voice flat with underlying anger Trent said, 'OK, OK, so you had no way of knowing she was frightened of water—you could have listened to her and not waited until she panicked.'

Rafe quavered, 'Will she be all right? Nicola, I'm sorry.'

'Save the apologies until tomorrow,' Trent said roughly. 'I'm taking her up to the cabin. And make sure the fire's out before you leave the beach.'

Karen said, 'Do you want me to come too, Nicola?'

But Nicola could not find her voice through the pain in her chest. Trent said more gently, 'If she needs you, I'll come and get you, Karen—thanks.'

Then the voices fell away and Trent and Nicola were alone, Trent tramping through the trees as though her weight was nothing to him. Infinitely grateful that every step was carrying her further away from the water, Nicola sagged against his chest, her fingers clutching his shirt pocket as though it were a lifeline. Her lungs were still shuddering for air and the cold of the sea seemed to have penetrated her very bones; like a tiny animal she huddled for warmth into his body.

She was quite unaware of whose side of the cabin he took her to, scarcely aware of him seating her on a chesterfield to strip off her clothes and rub her cold flesh with a thick towel. Then he had dressed her in a wool shirt and a pair of fleece-lined sweat pants and wrapped her in a blanket. He said clearly, as if he were speaking to a very young child, 'I'm going to put the hotplate on and make you a drink, Nicola, and then I'm going to get out of my wet clothes—I won't be long.'

She clutched the soft folds of the blanket to her chin, leaned against the back of the chesterfield, and closed her eyes. But when she did so, the blackness behind her lids became the blackness of the water, and she jerked them open again. It was Trent's room she was in, she thought confusedly. Of course it was. She was wearing his clothes, she was wrapped in his blanket. The blanket was blue; the extra blanket in her bedroom was green. If only she could stop shivering...

She had no idea how much time passed before Trent came back in the room. He was wearing dry jeans and a red checked shirt, clothes of no particular distinction in which he looked absolutely his own man, and he was carrying two steaming mugs. 'Hot milk and brandy,' he said. 'My grandmother had a gardener whose wife swore by hot milk and brandy for everything from toothache to childbirth.' He gave her a crooked smile. 'It can't hurt, Nicola.'

When he passed her the mug, her hands were shaking too much to hold it. He put his own down, cupped her palms around it and held them there with his own. 'Try it,' he said.

Although his gentleness touched her to the core, even then she did not cry. Wordlessly she took the first gulp of milk, and felt the brandy burn a path down her throat. Another mouthful and she was able to close her eyes, this time seeing only the bright checks of Trent's shirt dancing under her lids. Two more gulps and she whispered huskily, 'Thanks—I can manage now.'

By the time she had drained the mug, the worst of the shivering was over. Very slowly Nicola let her muscles relax into the warmth of the blanket; she put the empty mug on the arm of the chesterfield and looked over at Trent.

He was sitting at the other end of the chesterfield, one foot, clad in a wool sock, hooked underneath him, the leg of his jeans pulled taut over his thigh. He looked relaxed, she thought slowly. Relaxed, yet paradoxically ready to spring. He gave her a sober smile and said, 'You look much better.'

'The gardener's wife scores again,' she joked weakly. 'Trent, thank you for getting me out of the water.'

'I'm sorry it took me so long to realise what was going on—that what had started out as a bit of light-hearted fooling had turned into something much more serious. And I'm sorry, too, that I had to hit you.'

Her eyes fell. 'I thought you were Daniel, going to throw me back in the water again.'

'Why are you so frightened of it, Nicola?'

Subconsciously she had known this question was coming. She raised a troubled face, giving Trent a long, wordless look. He deserved the truth, didn't he? Because he had saved her from more than the cold waters of the bay; he had saved her from a mind-destroying fear whose roots went back to her childhood. And then, once he had rescued her, he had behaved in a way quite different from what she might have expected. He had taken off her wet clothes and rubbed her dry with as little emotion as if she had been a boy, and he had made no motions towards warming her naked body with his own. She was even sure he had brought her to his side of the cabin simply because he knew his way around in it, and could therefore tend to her more efficiently. No ulterior motives. No seizing of an unexpected opportunity to get her in his bed.

Yet he wanted her. Deny it though she might, his talk of seduction had not been just talk; Trent wanted her in the most basic way a man could want a woman.

Nicola huddled into the blanket and, staring straight ahead of her at the opposite wall, said in a strained voice, 'When I was seven I went out sailing one afternoon with my mother and father. My sisters didn't go because they'd been invited to a party. My father was a classics professor at the university, and new to sailing. He went out too far, and then the wind came up and we capsized. He managed to push me up on to the keel of the boat. But he wasn't wearing a life jacket and he drowned, and my mother died of the cold before we were rescued.'

Turning her head she looked over at Trent, her eyes dry of tears, her voice still devoid of emotion. 'I haven't gone swimming, or out in a boat, since then. I can't bear to.'

It would have been easy enough for Trent to fill in all the details she had left out: the howling wind and driven spray, the pounding waves washing over the capsized yacht where a little girl clung to the hull with frozen fingers as first her father, then her mother died in front of her eyes. Trent leaned over and took her, blanket and all, in his arms, rocking her back and forth. 'Nicola, I'm so sorry,' he said.

She resisted his embrace, pushing against it with her palms flat on his chest. 'It's a long time ago—sixteen years.' Producing a faint smile she added, 'And I cried enough tears those first few months to fill several oceans.'

He let go of her, not responding to her smile. 'That may be so. But you've been left with a terror of the water, haven't you?'

'That's understandable,' she flashed back.

'Of course. But scarcely healthy.'

Her mouth compressed, for she did not like his choice of words. 'Well, there's nothing I can do about it.'

He hesitated as if he were making a decision, then said slowly, 'There's something *we* could do about it.'

'No, there's not!'

'Just give me the chance to explain,' Trent said with commendable patience. 'I'm a good swimmer. And we're stuck here for the rest of the summer surrounded by any number of bodies of water. Lakes, rivers, fjords and bays. Why don't we have a swimming lesson every day the weather's fit for it?'

'I've been able to swim since the age of four,' Nicola replied with dangerous calm. 'That's not the problem.'

'So you do admit there's a problem.'

'You're putting words into my mouth! I don't want swimming lessons, Trent—I'm scared of the water.'

'Listen to me,' he said in a steel-edged voice. 'I know something about being scared, and how it can cripple you. Together we could conquer your fear, I know we could.'

'So what are *you* afraid of?'

His eyes held hers without wavering. 'Let's stick to one thing at a time, shall we—your fear of the water? If we work together, we can overcome it.' He raised his brow, his face suddenly full of laughter. 'I dare you to try.'

'No,' she said.

'Nicola, listen to me. You're not a coward because of your fear of the water—but you are a coward if you refuse to do anything about it.'

'Stop preaching,' she seethed. 'I've said no. I mean no.' Throwing back the folds of the blanket, she stood up. But Trent's sweat pants had not been designed with her in mind; hurriedly she clutched at the waistband and nearly tripped over the ankles. 'Damnation!' she cried. 'Why do we always end up yelling at each other?'

'I'm not yelling,' Trent said equably.

'Then why do I yell at you so much? Ever since the first time I met you.'

'That's for you to figure out.' He got to his feet with lazy grace. 'Think I should carry you home? I'd hate for you to break a leg so soon after nearly drowning.'

'I'm sure I can manage,' she said, hoisting the pants up as she began hobbling towards the door.

'You need to roll them up at the ankles,' Trent remarked, amusement deepening his voice.

'I wouldn't be answerable for the consequences if I let go of the waistband,' she responded tartly.

'Neither would I. Hold still a moment.' He knelt at her feet, rolling up the hems of the sweat pants until they were above her ankles. Nicola gazed down at his bent head with its sheaf of thick blond hair and felt again that fierce, melting hunger that was so disturbing, so vital, and so new. He stood up, keeping a careful distance between them as he grinned down at her. 'Your safety and your virtue are both protected and I have the feeling I'm a fool...sleep well, Nicola.'

Thoroughly confused, because part of her very much wanted to respond to the devilment in his eyes, Nicola blurted, 'I don't understand you. I don't understand myself when I'm around you.'

'Good. Think about the swimming lessons, won't you? Goodnight.'

Suddenly irritated out of all proportion, she snapped, 'You can't wait to get rid of me, can you?'

'There are limits to my self-control.'

But his slow smile, his loosely knit body, belied his words. 'Huh!' she said, glaring at him. 'It's privacy you want. Not me.'

'Yes?' He advanced on her, and although Nicola stood her ground, she quailed inwardly. But all he did when he got level with her was to reach around her to open the screen door. 'Goodnight, Nicola,' he said calmly.

It was difficult to look dignified when wearing sweat pants that sagged around her hips and a shirt whose sleeves dangled below her wrists, but Nicola did her best. She stalked through the door and down the steps in her bare feet and before she reached the bottom step heard both the screen and the inner door close softly behind her.

To hell with you, Trent Livingstone, she raged, her bare soles slapping up her own stairs. And to hell with your swimming lessons. I *know* how to swim. And I don't need you trying to run my life and tell me what's good for me.

Any more than I need you pushing me out of your cabin with such indecent haste.

As soon as she was in her bedroom, Nicola dragged off Trent's clothes, letting them lie on the floor in an untidy heap. She hauled on a warm nightgown and fell into bed, the springs squeaking in protest. From the other side of the wall a deep voice said, 'You have an awful temper, Nicola.'

Nicola pulled the covers over her head. He was a horrible man and she hated him and she was going to have nothing to do with him for the rest of the summer.

With the suddenness of an exhausted child, she fell asleep.

CHAPTER SIX

FLINT behaved himself admirably the next morning, his mocking smile, his lazy grace, his quizzically raised brow so wonderfully clear to Nicola that the words tripped from her brain to the computer screen. Maryanne was certainly enjoying the change; she had only been half alive with the estimable but dull Jonathan, Nicola now realised. By afternoon Nicola had finished the first chapter, and when she read through the print-out she found herself amazed that she, Nicola, had actually written these words.

She was also fascinated by the way Flint had evolved as a character in less than thirty pages. Although he might originally have been inspired by Trent, he was no carbon copy, and already was taking on a definite life of his own. Nicola was very glad of this. It would have been poor thanks to Trent after he had rescued her from the icy waters of the bay to have used him as her hero in a work of fiction; and her initial motive of revenge was something she was now thoroughly ashamed of.

She typed 'Chapter Two' at the top of the screen, wondering if she wasn't a little bit in love with Flint herself, and plunged into the next scene.

This scene, however, was a little more difficult, for it necessitated a sizzling description of Flint and Maryanne meeting at the side of the pool in the resort where they were staying, Flint in brief navy swimming trunks and Maryanne in a bikini. Scowling at the screen, Nicola worked her way into the scene line by line, letting her imagination wander among all kinds of possibilities as

Maryanne and Flint fenced with each other in the sunshine. Then, suddenly, Flint and Maryanne were speaking instead of Nicola, and her fingers began dancing across the keys. When she went to dinner she was well pleased with her afternoon's work and had no problem allowing herself a second helping of strawberry shortcake.

After the meal Rafe and Daniel—both of whom had avoided her all day—took her aside for an apology none the less sincere for obviously having been rehearsed, and to show them that she harboured no ill feelings she went for a walk with them along the shore to watch the seals lying on the rocks at low tide.

Daniel sighted an eagle and started taking pictures; Rafe was jotting down notes. Nicola sat quietly on a rough chunk of granite, gazing at the peaceful inlet glazed with the pale pinks and golds of the evening sky. A gull swooped low on arched wings, almost meeting its own shadow in the water. Water that she was afraid of.

Was Trent right? Was she a coward to nurse her fear, to avoid having anything to do with the water or boats for sixteen years? She had never been able to go to pool parties or to the beach with her friends; she had always produced an excuse and after a while they had stopped inviting her. But now Trent was giving her the chance to change all that. And she had turned him down. Because she was afraid.

She went to bed in a thoughtful mood that night, and woke to a crisp sunny morning with a playful breeze that ruffled her hair and gossiped among the birch leaves as she walked to the dining-room for breakfast. Afterwards, she put in a solid three hours of work, and when she turned off the computer knew that without being consciously aware of her thought processes she had made a decision. Leaving the cabin, she went looking for Trent.

TAKE FOUR
BEST SELLER ROMANCES
FREE!

♥

Best Sellers are for the true romantic! These stories are our favourite Romance titles re-published by popular demand.

♥

And to introduce to you this superb series, we'll send you four Best Sellers absolutely FREE when you complete and return this card.

♥

We're so confident that you will enjoy Best Sellers that we'll also reserve a subscription for you to the Mills & Boon Reader Service, which means you could enjoy...

♥

Mills & Boon

Four new novels
sent direct to you every two months (before they're available in the shops).

Free postage and packing
we pay all the extras.

Free regular Newsletter
packed with special offers, competitions, author news and much, much more.

Mills & Boon FREE BOOKS CERTIFICATE

YES! Please send me my four **FREE** Best Sellers together with my **FREE** gifts. Please also reserve me a special Reader Service Subscription. If I decide to subscribe, I shall receive four superb Best Sellers every other month for just £6 postage and packing free. If I decide not to subscribe I shall write to you within 10 days. Any **FREE** books and gifts will remain mine to keep. I understand that I am under no obligation whatsoever - I may cancel or suspend my subscription at any time simply by writing to you. *I am over 18 years of age.*   6AIB

NAME ——————————— Signature ———————

ADDRESS ———————————————————————

——————————————— POSTCODE ——————

► **POST TODAY**
and we'll send you this
cuddly Teddy Bear.

**PLUS a free
mystery gift!**
we all love mysteries, so as
well as the FREE books and
cuddly Teddy, there's an
intriguing mystery gift
specially for you.

MILLS & BOON
FREEPOST
P.O. BOX 236
CROYDON
CR9 9EL

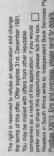

The lunch bell had not yet chimed, so he would surely be somewhere on the grounds.

The cedar bushes had all gone, the ground dug up around the roots; the perennial borders behind the house were weeded and staked into rigid tidiness and the herb garden that was enclosed by a privet hedge had been recently hoed. But there was no sign of Trent. Then Nicola passed through a gap in the hedge to the vegetable garden, the only occupants of which were two barrel-chested robins rooting for worms, and heard the sound of clippers.

She rounded the far hedge. Another privet hedge, tall and unkempt, surrounded a small fountain and a rather attractive rock garden, and it was the top of this hedge that Trent was engaged in clipping. From it he had shaped a fat dove to guard the entrance and a recognisable peacock to perch at one corner, and he was observing, head to one side, the rather chubby bird that was taking shape between these two. Nicola burst out laughing.

His head turned. 'It's always been the fate of genius to be derided by lesser mortals,' he said.

She gave the chubby bird a closer scrutiny. 'I see what it is! It's a turkey.'

'No, Nicola. It's an eagle.'

'Oops.' Her eyes brimming with laughter she said, 'I trust Olivia is paying you more than minimum wage for this outburst of creativity.'

'As a true artist I have a soul above money.' Trent gave the wide grin that Nicola found so attractive. 'Plus, I might as well tell you, regular gardening bores me to tears.'

'I'd noticed that.' Before she could lose her courage, she said rapidly, 'I hope I won't be adding to your boredom if I take you up on your offer of swimming lessons.'

Quite another emotion gleamed behind the blue eyes. 'On the contrary,' he said suavely.

She hated it when she had no idea what he was thinking. 'If you still want to, that is,' she muttered.

'I'll meet you at the cabin at four, and we'll be back in time for dinner.'

'Today?' she gasped.

'Before you change your mind again.'

'I haven't got a swimsuit!'

'You won't need one today; wear your shorts. I have to go to Corner Brook again for Olivia on Thursday—I'll pick you up one. Or better still, you could take a day off and come with me.'

'I see why you're bored with gardening,' Nicola said with asperity. 'Plants grow at their own speed and in their own season and there's very little you can do to hurry them up. Whereas you're a mover, Trent. You'd want delphiniums blooming in May and chrysanthemums in July.'

'Don't they?' he said innocently.

She raised her eyes heavenwards. 'I'll be ready at four,' she said, and made her escape.

But by four o'clock Nicola was a mass of nerves. When Trent rapped on her door, dressed in ragged-edged shorts that had once been a pair of jeans, and a grey T-shirt, a towel draped over one shoulder, she announced, 'I don't want to go,' and braced herself to resist his anger.

But once again he surprised her. His face very serious, he said, 'I'm sure you don't. After all, why should you? You have no idea what we're going to do, and very little basis for trusting me. But I want you to trust me, Nicola. I promise we won't do anything you don't want to do; there'll be no tricks, no gimmicks, certainly nothing on the same level with what Daniel and Rafe did. And if in two weeks you don't see any progress, then we'll quit. With no hard feelings.'

She gazed at him in perplexity. There was not a trace of anger in his face, and none of the mockery she had come to expect; he spoke with such conviction that she found herself almost believing him. 'All right,' she said faintly.

'Good. The truck's parked near the house.'

'Aren't we going to the shore?'

'No. There's a lake I know where you have to walk out for almost a quarter of a mile before the water's over your head. And there won't be anyone watching.'

He had thought of everything. 'You probably could make delphiniums bloom in May,' she said even more faintly.

'Next May I don't want to be within ten miles of a goddamned delphinium,' was the grim response.

Frustration. Tamped down energy. Nicola saw them both, and was aware of an emotion in herself that could have been compassion. But she knew better than to ask questions. Instead she hooked her arm into his and said, 'To the lake. If in two weeks you can have me swimming in water over my head, the delphiniums can bloom whenever they like.'

Her fingers were resting as lightly as a butterfly on his wrist. He looked down at them, a strange expression on his face. 'Thanks, Nicola,' he said huskily. Then he raised her hand to his lips and kissed the softness of her palm.

The brief caress—for he had let go of her hand as soon as he raised his head—shot through her like a shaft of flame. But Trent was already striding across the grass towards the trees. Nicola stumbled after him, quite sure that she was mad. Bad enough that she had pledged to confront her deepest fear with the help of a man she scarcely knew. Even worse that that man had only to touch her for her to dissolve into inchoate desire.

She would be alone with him every day for two weeks on the shore of an isolated lake. What on earth was she thinking of?

Two weeks passed, day by day, and gradually Nicola came to the conclusion that she must have dreamed that brief caress by the cabin door; certainly she had been a fool to worry that Trent would take advantage of the isolation of the lake to seduce her. He showed not the slightest interest in seducing her. He had, of necessity, to touch her sometimes in the course of their lessons, but he did so with such impersonality that her flesh was chilled.

She had been mistaken to think that he wanted her. Or else he had changed his mind.

Nicola buried some of her hurt deep in her subconscious and got rid of the rest of it in the entangled and incendiary relationship between Maryanne and Flint; a Flint, she was pleased to notice, who hardly resembled Trent at all. And in the meantime, wearing a swimsuit she had borrowed from Karen, for she had declined to take a day off and go to Corner Brook with Trent, she worked as hard at the lake as she was working at the computer. She sat in the water. She put her face in it. She dunked her head under and opened her eyes. She lay back and let Trent tow her. And each day she went a little deeper, with a little more confidence and a little less fear, until finally on the fourteenth day she swam fifty feet out into the lake in water over her head, and then swam back, Trent keeping pace only a few feet away from her.

Nicola let her feet touch bottom and stood up, shaking the water from her hair. 'I did it,' she said in wonderment. 'Trent, I did it! I swam in deep water and I didn't panic.'

He stood up too, his body hair slicked to his chest, water running in little streams down his flat belly. His eyes dancing, he held out one hand. 'Congratulations, Nicola,' he said.

With one of the stabs of pain that she had almost got used to she knew that what she really wanted to do was fling herself in his arms rather than politely shake his hand. But Nicola had her share of pride; she took the proffered hand in her own, clasped it strongly, and said with all the intensity she was capable of, 'Trent, I can't thank you enough. It's like a miracle—I never expected I could do it. Even yesterday I didn't think I could.' She gave him a generous smile, her eyes sparkling. 'But you knew I could, didn't you?'

'I thought you could.' He squeezed her hand. 'It's nice of you to thank me. But you're the one who did it, Nicola. You stuck with it, you did things you were scared to do, and all along you trusted me—don't think I didn't see how difficult it was for you sometimes, and how much courage you showed.' He smiled at her crookedly. 'I learned a lot about you the last two weeks.'

Her eyes were suddenly flooded with tears that mingled with the lakewater on her lashes. She would cherish his words forever, she thought helplessly, for he had seen beyond the façade she showed the world to the real Nicola. Then she felt him release her hand. From somewhere she dredged up more courage, the courage to say steadily, with no hint of the turmoil in her heart, 'Could I go for one more swim, do you think? Before we go back?'

'Sure. I think we should come here once or twice more and then have two or three session at the beach. When you can swim straight out into the bay I figure it'll be time for me to retire.'

Which meant she would no longer have these outings as a fixed part of her day. A part she looked forward to, Nicola thought, striking out into the lake with a chill of fear that had nothing to do with the water. Somehow over the last two weeks Trent had become very important to her. For if she had shown courage and persistence, he had shown patience and humour and ingenuity. Most important of all, he had believed in her.

Stroking out vigorously, forgetting that the water beneath her was deep and that two weeks ago she could not have done this, Nicola let her thoughts carry her forwards. She had learned during these swimming lessons that Trent could be trustworthy and caring and fun. Without her noticing quite how it had happened, he had become her friend.

But that was all he was. Because he did not want to be anything else.

He did not want to be her lover. He had behaved more like a brother than a lover the last few days, and those few times, that now seemed so long ago, when he had kissed her and told her she was exquisite, had disappeared as if they had never been. And she had no idea why.

Churning up the water, she swam further than she had ever done before, and when she got back to shore she was out of breath. 'We'll be late for supper,' she panted, pulling on a loose shirt over her swimsuit.

'All in a good cause,' Trent said casually, and just as casually drove her back to the Eyrie.

They were ten minutes late for the evening meal; after supper Nicola had an appointment with Olivia, to whom she had already given the first two chapters in which Flint had usurped Jonathan, and a third chapter as well.

Olivia was wearing a rather peculiar garment made of silk hand-painted with what looked like an octopus. Her hairdo writhed like Medusa's snakes and her jewellery, chrome-plated, jangled and clanked. She waved one arm enthusiastically through the air, to the peril of the potted fern by her desk, and said, 'Nicola! This affair with Trent has done you the world of good. It's loosened up your writing, freed your emotions—I knew that's what would happen.' She smiled rather smugly at Nicola and added impatiently, 'Sit down, girl—don't wait to be asked.'

Nicola, still standing, said crisply, 'What affair?'

'Now, Nicola, you don't have to be coy with me.' Olivia leaned over the desk. 'Swimming lessons! Rather a clever ploy, I suppose, but not one that would deceive *me* for long. I really must congratulate you, I didn't think you had it in you.'

It was the second time Nicola had been congratulated that day. Aware that she was quite astoundingly angry, she snapped, 'Your were right—I don't have it in me. The swimming lessons have been exactly that, and nothing more.'

'So you don't want to talk about it...I do understand. Although,' and Olivia's eyes glittered naughtily, 'in creating Flint you're giving it all away anyway.'

Nicola sat down with a thud, her nostrils flared. 'Olivia, the plain truth is that Trent does not want an affair with me! As far as I can tell he could have been steering a wooden chair around the lake for the last two weeks.' She took a deep breath, glared into one of the mean little eyes of the octopus, and said, 'Now—what about the book?'

'The book is marvellous. You're on the right track and that's all there is to say.' Olivia gave her a thoughtful look. 'I do believe you're telling the truth.'

'Of course I am,' Nicola exclaimed, and fought back a ridiculous urge to burst into tears.

'Then it's time we did something about that. Come along.' And Olivia got to her feet.

'Come where?' Nicola said warily.

'Up to my apartment.' Olivia directed a scathing look at Nicola's plain white T-shirt and faded jeans. 'It's a brightly coloured flower that attracts the bee.'

'Trent doesn't like flowers,' Nicola said trenchantly, and threw out her next words as a challenge. 'Which is funny for a gardener.'

'Mmmph,' said Olivia.

'And what does *that* mean?'

'Never you mind, child. Now let's see what we can do about this anachronistic virginity of yours.' In a flurry of tentacles Olivia marched around the desk and swept through the door. Nicola let out an exasperated sigh and followed; for under the exasperation she was nursing the warm glow that Olivia's praise had brought, a warm glow that enabled her to sit quietly under Olivia's ministrations for the next hour, perhaps not giving them the attention she should have. The book was good. Olivia had said so, and in this matter Nicola was prepared to trust Olivia's judgement. Dreamily, hardly aware of Olivia poking and prodding her into yet another outfit, she began to plan a scene on the beach for the next chapter.

Finally Olivia said, 'Now—go look at yourself in the mirror and tell me you won't knock Trent off his feet.'

Obediently Nicola tottered in what appeared to be very high heels over to the gilt-scrolled mirror, and glanced at her own reflection. Her eyes, already exaggerated by false lashes and a generous palette of eyeshadow, widened in dismay. She did not look like Nicola at all.

She looked like a shorter, brown-haired version of Olivia. She looked awful.

Flint, who had been about to draw Maryanne into his arms on the white sand, dropped from her mind, to be replaced by a Trent who would most certainly be knocked off his feet. Not from stunned admiration, as Olivia was assuming. From horror. Or, worse, laughter.

Her hair, which had grown since she had come to the Eyrie had been teased into as many curls as Olivia could produce. Her cheeks were twin patches of fuchsia, her lips fuchsia slashes, and her throat reeked of perfume, while her dress, on the streets of St John's, would have had her arrested for solicitation. The top was pale grey chiffon, through which Nicola's nipples showed; she had not been wearing a bra under her white T-shirt. The skirt, of fuchsia silk, was slit to the top of one thigh. Her shoes, also fuchsia, had heels that would trip a gazelle.

Said Olivia, obviously interpreting Nicola's silence quite the wrong way, 'Duckling to swan, darling. Amazing, isn't it, what a difference a little make-up and the right clothes can make?'

Belatedly Nicola found her voice. 'It certainly is,' she said, and fumbled for the buttons on the blouse. There were only two, each almost at waist level.

'What are you doing?' Olivia asked sharply.

'I'm taking this off.'

'You can't! I want Trent to see you.'

Nicola abandoned the buttons and struggled for tact. 'Olivia, you look great in clothes like this,' she said. 'They work on you. They suit you. But they don't suit me. Maybe I'm not a duckling. But I'm not a flamingo, either. I can't go back to the cabin looking like this! I'll keep the make-up on if that will make you feel better, and I really do appreciate the trouble you've taken—but I'm putting my own clothes back on.'

Olivia raised pencilled brows, gathered Nicola's shirt and jeans under her arm, and headed for the door. Over her shoulder she said, 'You won't be able to, will you?'

Open-mouthed, Nicola watched the door click shut behind her. She turned back to the mirror, shuddered, and ran for the door, the shoes cruelly pinching her feet. 'Olivia,' she called. 'Come back here!'

Dead silence. Nicola pulled the door open and looked down the long carpeted hallway. Four doors, all closed, and the one Olivia was hiding behind undoubtedly locked. 'Olivia!' she shouted. 'You can't *do* this!'

A voice floated down the hall. 'Oh, yes, I can. Go home and finish chapter four, Nicola.'

Nicola said a pungent word under her breath and tried to think. There were metal stairs at the back of the house—she had seen them through the kitchen windows and assumed them to be a fire escape. If she sneaked down those and took a roundabout route to the cabin through the woods, no one would see her.

What other choice did she have?

She looked down at the fuchsia shoes with distaste. She would have to keep them on, because a wide gravelled driveway stretched behind the house, and rocks and roots floored the woods. Inwardly vowing all manner of vengeance on Olivia, she hitched up her skirt and went to her left down the hallway. A door with an inside latch led her out on to a metal platform at the head of a steep flight of stairs. Holding tightly to the railing, praying no one would see her, Nicola began her descent.

It was dark; for that she was grateful. The kitchen windows were unlit and the driveway deserted. After tiptoeing across the gravel she scurried into the scented darkness of the trees like a squirrel gone to ground.

There was not a breath of wind. The tiny scufflings and scrapes of the fuchsia shoes sounded very loud and she had to fight the tendency to look nervously back over her shoulder. A tree root caught the pointed toe of one shoe so that she nearly pitched face forward; catching at the nearest trunk she scraped her palm on a spiked branch and the imagined vengeance against Olivia became a little more lurid. Clutching the wounded palm in her other hand, she saw an angled dark line cutting into the starred darkness of the sky; the roofline of the cabin, she thought in great relief, and stumbled towards it through the last of the trees.

But at the edge of the pines, she stopped. The lights were on in Trent's side of the cabin, the side nearest her, and none of the curtains were drawn. Trent was the last person she wanted seeing her guyed up like some kind of cheap, trashy doll. She frowned in thought. If she took off her shoes, ducked low and ran for her own side of the cabin, then crept up the steps as quietly as she could, she would be all right. Edging free of a low-hanging bough, she bent to remove the shoes, which were, she noticed with a grimace, so tight they had bitten into her instep. As she did so, her breasts almost fell out of her blouse. Her excuse for a blouse, she amended wryly.

Then, as though the director of a film had just called for action, the light over Trent's door went on, Trent pushed the screen open, and stepped outside. His head jerked in her direction. 'Who's that?' he demanded.

Wishing the ground would open and swallow her up, Nicola straightened, one shoe on, one off, and crossed her arms over her chest. After the seclusion of the woods, the light glared in her eyes; every detail of her appearance must be clear to him, she thought sickly. Struggling to find the courage he had so admired in her, she faltered,

'It's me—Nicola. Trent, if you have any liking for me at all, go back inside and forget you ever saw me like this. Please.'

Very slowly he descended the four stairs and started across the grass towards her. 'I don't think so...' he said, his eyes narrowing in disbelief as he got closer to her. 'My God, Nicola, what have you done to yourself?'

I will not cry, she thought. I will not. Her throat tight, the false lashes wavering across her vision like spider legs, she struggled to find the words, any words, that could explain her predicament. Olivia thought this would induce you to have an affair with me? That was the truth, but she could hardly say it. Olivia thinks I'm a poor excuse for a woman? Not much better.

Struck dumb, she watched his eyes travel from her fluffed-up hair to the single fuchsia shoe, not missing, she was sure, one detail on the way. He said flatly, 'What are you trying to do, look like Suzie?'

She remembered Suzie's sensual, bare-footed dance on the beach and knew with a kind of desperation that she could not keep the tears back much longer. With the speed of a trapped animal she grabbed her skirt and lunged towards the cabin.

But Trent grabbed her arm, swinging her off balance. The heel of her one remaining shoe caught in the long grass, and she would have fallen had he not quickly circled her waist with his other hand. Nicola struck out at him, tears abandoned in a sudden, overwhelming flood of rage. 'Don't touch me!' she spat.

Her breasts, small, firm, pointed, gleamed through the grey chiffon, her nipples dark shadows; her eyes were liquid with anger. His own darkened with purpose. Pulling her against the length of his body, he kissed her hard on the mouth.

Rage and desire fused into a burst of fire. Subconsciously Nicola had been waiting for this kiss for two weeks, and into it she put all her pent-up frustration and newly found, passionately felt hunger. Her arms slid up to circle his neck, her fingers linking themselves in his thick, soft hair. Of her own volition her body melted into his, pliant as the long grass, fierce as a shaft of flame.

His teeth nibbled gently at her lower lip, teasing her, tantalising her, until with a tiny sound that was both protest and surrender her lips parted. His kiss deepened. With one hand he was stroking the curve of her back, his palm warm through the thin chiffon; the other traced the concavity of her waist, the swell of her hip, and then found the silky skin of her thigh where the skirt parted. He pulled his head free long enough to mutter her name, his mouth tasting the long taut line of her throat and burying itself in the soft hollow at its base. Nicola clutched his shoulders, her heart racing in her breast. And then, with a wonderment that surged through her like a tide of the sea, she felt his arousal.

He wanted her. Trent wanted her.

She pushed against his chest with the flats of her hands, wanting to look into his eyes and share the joy of this mutual discovery. To tell him how naturally and how beautifully he had awakened her sexuality, and how new and wonderful this all was to her. However, as if her action had been the signal he had been waiting for, Trent suddenly straightened, dropping his hands. His breathing hoarse, he said unevenly, 'Now—why don't you answer the question, Nicola? What the devil are you doing in that get-up?'

He flicked the collar of the blouse with a contemptuous finger. Nicola gripped a handful of his shirt—a blue denim shirt, she noticed dazedly—to prevent herself from losing her balance, and said with the honesty of shock, 'My outfit isn't what I need to talk about. Not right now.'

'Who are you kidding? That outfit is a come-on if ever I saw one. So who have you been with, Nicola? Who are you after? Are you trying to act like Suzie as well as look like her, is that it?'

Her mouth gaped open. 'You think I'm like Suzie? Desperate for a man, and any man will do?'

'Look at you—you might as well be naked. More honest, perhaps, if you were.'

Like a kettle that suddenly boiled over, Nicola lost her temper. Drawing herself up to her full height, not altogether easy in view of her one shoe, she looked Trent full in the eye and said, 'Olivia dressed me up like this, like some kind of a doll you'd win at a fair. When I told her—oh, ever so tactfully—that I didn't think it was quite my style, she locked herself in another room along with all my clothes. And do you know what her motive was, Trent Livingstone?' Beyond any notion of caution or restraint, Nicola poked him in the chest for emphasis and did not wait for a reply. 'I'll tell you what it was! She thinks I'm not half the woman Suzie is. She thinks if I walk into you in a skirt that's slit to the navel and a blouse unbuttoned to the navel you'll have an affair with me, and then I'll write a better book. *That's* why I'm going around looking like an escapee from a Hallowe'en party.'

She had run out of words, but her eyes still blazed with anger and her chiffon-draped breast was heaving with emotion. There was a long, charged silence, which she eventually broke by saying irritably, 'For heaven's sake, say something.'

In a hard voice Trent said, 'Do you want to have an affair with me——'

'No! I don't know. How can I know?' Nicola sputtered.

'—so you'll write a better book?'

'I'm writing a very good book without having an affair with anyone, thank you very much,' she said roundly.

'Good. I'm glad that's out of the way.' Then Trent added reflectively, 'Olivia's no fool. Like me, she's picked up on your—dammit, I hate to use words like inferiority complex, I sound like a textbook. You doubt yourself, Nicola. At some deep level you're afraid to admit you're a very beautiful young woman... is it something to do with the two men you told me about?'

That, thought Nicola, and growing up with two older, highly charged sisters. 'I talk too much,' she said.

'You don't talk enough.'

'Well, I'm certainly not going to stand here in a blouse that'll give me pneumonia and a shoe that'll permanently cripple me and tell you my life story,' she pronounced, tossing her head and catching a strong whiff of perfume as she did so. 'I stink,' she added succinctly.

'You do, rather. Take off your other shoe and you can have my shirt, and give me the abridged version.'

He was unbuttoning his shirt while he spoke. Alarm bells going off in her head, Nicola saw the broad expanse of his chest as he shrugged out of the blue shirt, and the fading scar on his arm that was nothing like a rope burn, and then felt the warmth from his body as he put the shirt over her shoulders. She pulled it round her to cover her breasts and said uncertainly, 'You'll get cold.'

He put his hands in the pockets of his jeans, rocking gently on the balls of his feet. 'No, I won't. You can start any time. *Why I Avoid Men*. By Nicola Shea.'

Clutching both her blouse and the shirt to maintain some semblance of decency, she bent down and removed the second shoe, keeping it in her hand and regarding it pensively. 'Not a bad weapon of defence,' she said. 'Or offence.'

'Chapter One, Nicola.'

'I don't know why I should tell you . . . I've never told anyone else.'

'Because you trust me.'

'I trust you in the middle of a lake,' she responded pithily. 'But I'm not so sure about here and now.'

'Give—because you know as well as I do that you're afraid of more than water.'

She was. Of course. Olivia had seen that as well. With something of the same tightness in her chest that she had felt when she had first walked into the lake, Nicola said, 'This is about my sisters more than about me. Gayle and Cheryl. Five and three years older than me chronologically, aeons older in terms of what counts. They're like Suzie. They attract men without even trying, flocks of men, dozens of men—they don't even think about it, they take it for granted. They're beautiful, they're sexy, they're like honey to a bee . . .' Nicola wriggled her shoulders inside the denim shirt. 'Are you sure you want to hear all this?'

'Two men came along whom *you* wanted and Gayle and Cheryl snaffled them from under your nose.'

'Not a great plot,' Nicola concurred. 'Yes, that's what happened. When I was nineteen, I took a secretarial course and went to work at a doctor's office. Soon afterwards I started dating George Mowbery, the new young doctor in town. I fell in love with him, and he said he loved me, too. And then Gayle came home from Halifax for a visit, and he took one look at her and it was as if I didn't even exist.' She ducked her head. 'I was devastated.'

'But not surprised,' Trent said gently.

'Not really. It had always been that way. Gran used to tell people that she never had to worry about *me* as far as boys were concerned, I was such a quiet little thing. Pretty enough, she supposed, but not like Gayle and Cheryl. She worried about them all the time. She enjoyed it, I think.'

'Did your grandmother never really look at you?'

Although he had spoken quietly, Nicola knew him well enough to know he was angry. 'Maybe not,' she said briefly. 'Anyway, after Gran died I used the money she had left me to go to university in St John's, to study English. In my second year I met Allan, he was doing a graduate degree in philosophy—and I fell in love again. This time we got engaged. And then Cheryl arrived one day and fluttered her lashes and kissed him on the cheek to welcome him to the family and I watched it happen all over again. His eyes got dazed, he could hardly talk, he followed her everywhere she went like a puppy on a leash.' Nicola scowled at the fuchsia shoe in her hand. 'So I broke the engagement. What else could I do? The worst part was that Cheryl didn't even realise what she had done... neither of my sisters is mean, or purposely out to wreck my life. It just—happens.'

'So now you don't believe you can possibly be desirable to a man. Or if you are, it's just temporary, until someone sexier comes along.'

She shrugged. 'After George and I broke up I decided, if you can't beat 'em, join 'em. So I went through a phase of wearing more ruffles than a southern belle and more curls than a judge's wig. I simpered. I prattled. I bought false eyelashes—not quite as false as these— and waggled them at anything male over the age of sixteen.'

'What happened?'

'Nothing very much. George proposed to Gayle who turned him down, after which he switched practices to a different office. My way of dealing with that was to have a punk stage. Turquoise hair, black leather and army boots. I attracted men then, I can tell you.'

'But all the wrong kind.'

'Certainly no one I could take home to Gran.'

'So then you went to university, where I bet you studied your head off every day of the week. When are you going to take a good long look at yourself in the mirror, Nicola?'

She gazed up at him, her face troubled under the garish make-up. 'It's only lately that I've wondered if either George or Allan was the right man for me,' she confessed in a rush.

'I would suspect you ought to be down on your knees thanking your sisters. Did George and Allan know you were afraid of water and had a grandmother who didn't value you nearly as highly as your sisters?'

'Gran changed her mind,' Nicola said quickly. 'When I was twenty I stayed with her for eight months—she had cancer—and before she died she told me how much she loved me.'

'That may be true. But perhaps by then the damage was done.' Trent rested his hands on her shoulders, his body so close she caught the clean soap-scent of his skin. 'Listen to me—you're beautiful and courageous and full of life. I want you to remember that. Repeat it ten times before breakfast if that's what it takes.'

When Trent looked at her with that unsettling combination of force and concern, Nicola did not think she would need to tell herself anything; it was all there in his eyes. Trent, she thought, was nothing like George or Allan. 'How did your grandmother treat you, Trent?' she asked softly.

His hands fell to his sides. 'I have my own demons,' he said heavily. 'Nothing to do with you ... I'd just like to see you take your place in the sun, Nicola.'

Obscurely disappointed, she whispered, 'So you're a friend—sort of like a big brother? Is that what you are?' She fumbled for the right words. 'All through the swimming lessons—it was as though I was a stick of wood.'

His bark of laughter was entirely unamused. 'You couldn't be further from the truth. But we made a deal for the duration of those lessons—no gimmicks, no fooling around. So I stuck to that deal.'

'Oh,' Nicola said with a smile of transparent relief. 'I never thought of that. I figured you didn't want me after all. That you really did see yourself as a big brother.'

'The way I kissed you was not at all brotherly.'

She had to agree. 'I don't understand you!' she cried, and knew she had used those words before.

'Look, I know how the past can sit like a great black bird on your shoulder.' He dredged up a smile. 'I'm just flapping my arms around so yours will fly away.'

She spoke without thinking. 'Can't I do the same for you, Trent?'

'It's claws are dug in too deep,' he said flatly. 'But thanks for offering.'

A light breeze stirred the pine boughs; she saw Trent shiver and was herself shaken by a fierce and all-encompassing compassion quite unlike anything she had ever felt for George or Allan. 'If you change your mind, I'm here,' she said steadily. 'Will you remember that?'

He leaned forward and dropped a kiss on the tip of her nose that would certainly have qualified as brotherly, then said, 'I came out to load up the truck with some stuff Olivia wants me to take to Deer Lake ... I'd better go, or she'll be wondering what we're up to. If she asks, I haven't seen you, OK?'

Nicola slipped the shirt from her shoulders and passed it to him, making no effort to cover her breasts as she stood straight and tall in the outlandish clothes. There was a new pride in her bearing and her brown eyes were very clear. 'OK,' she said.

Trent pulled the shirt on, opened his mouth to speak, shut it again, and gave her a tight smile that did not reach his eyes. Turning on his heel, he left the clearing. Nicola picked up her other shoe and padded across the grass to the cabin.

CHAPTER SEVEN

THE next day Maryanne, after a scorching scene on the beach, realised she was in love with Flint. Nicola reread the four pages she had just written; and then suddenly found herself going all through her manuscript changing Flint's hair from streaked blond to dark brown, and his eyes from blue to a sea-green. If she had been asked why she was doing this, she would have had a hard time coming up with a rational reason.

Because she was no longer the slightest bit in love with her hero? Was that it?

Or was it because Trent was becoming so much more real to her that she had to totally detach him from Flint? That she did not want Flint resembling Trent either outwardly or inwardly?

But I'm not in love with Trent any more than I'm in love with Flint, she thought in puzzlement.

No? queried a little voice in her head. You want to go to bed with him, don't bother denying that.

She couldn't. Just to imagine herself lying beside Trent, feeling his intense blue eyes travel over her naked body, made her weak with longing. But lust and love did not necessarily travel together, she'd read enough books to know that, and how could she love a man whose life was a mystery to her, whose very presence here at the Eyrie did not make sense?

Of course she didn't love Trent.

With considerable effort Nicola brought her mind back to Flint; and for the next three days drove herself unmercifully until she finished the fifth chapter and

Maryanne and Flint had become heart-rendingly estranged in a way she had no idea how to mend. She went to bed at midnight worrying about it, and woke up the next morning with no solution in sight.

Clumping down her steps, oblivious to the heat already trapped in the clearing, she wished Maryanne hadn't so thoroughly declared how much she hated Flint. But Maryanne had spoken from the heart, and the words could not be changed.

A voice broke into her reverie. 'You look as though you've lost your best friend.'

She frowned at Trent and said accusingly, 'I didn't hear you get up.'

'I couldn't sleep. I've been reading since five o'clock. What's your problem?'

'What kept you awake?'

He said evenly, 'I could hear you breathing on the other side of the wall.'

'Oh.' Nicola blushed. 'I know the feeling.'

'When are we going to do something about it, Nicola?'

'When we're both ready,' she said, and somehow knew that she had stated a profound truth.

He nodded, his eyes trained on her face. 'I guess you're right...so why were you looking so grumpy a few minutes ago?'

'My hero and heroine aren't speaking to each other and I don't know what to do about it. Dialogue,' she added ruefully, 'is essential to the book.'

'Send them off into the woods in a big storm and they'll end up making love,' Trent said promptly. 'That'll fix 'em.'

'The mood my heroine's in she'll push him in the creek,' Nicola said gloomily.

Trent laughed. 'You need a break! Tell you what, let's take the boat trip up the fjord today. It's only twenty miles from here.'

For the first time that morning she really looked at him. In blue shorts and a grass-stained T-shirt, he towered over her, the sun glinting in his hair, his eyes the colour of the sky. As her heart did a flip-flop worthy of Maryanne, Nicola was suddenly glad she was wearing shorts herself, brief white ones with a tailored green shirt and matching green sandals. Her tan wasn't in great shape, but one could not ask for everything.

She had heard about the cruise between the high cliffs of the fjord that had been carved by glaciers thousands of years ago. 'A big boat?' she said uncertainly.

'Thirty passengers, lifejackets, and me beside you—you'll be quite safe.'

To go out in a boat would be a true test of her newly found courage in the water; and who would she rather go with than Trent? 'Yes,' she said recklessly.

'I'll call up and get reservations. Wear jeans and good walking shoes, there's a forty-five-minute trek to the boat.' Then Trent's eyes gleamed with something other than sunlight. 'I like your shorts, Nicola...shall we go for breakfast?'

When he looked like that she knew why she had given Flint blond hair and blue eyes, although she would not have admitted this for the world. Nor did she want to admit how very much like Maryanne she felt when they set out in the truck two hours later: full of anticipation, eyes sparkling, happy.

By the time they had tramped through spruce woods stunted by the Atlantic winds, and across barrens wet with sphagnum moss and spiked with the stout red flowers of pitcher plants, portentous grey and white clouds had piled over the gash in the cliffs that was the entrance to the fjord. But at the wharf where the boat was being loaded there was a festive air and the water was mirror-smooth. Trent and Nicola climbed aboard, sat on the bench by the gunwales and ate the sandwiches and apples Trent had brought.

They set off, to a running commentary from the captain. Nicola had a bad moment when she first saw the water sliding smoothly along the sides of the boat, as though the wood were greased, to join in a churning wake at the stern. But she knew now that she could swim in that water if she had to, and besides, Trent had his arm casually around her shoulders; she gave him a smile as bright as the foam and felt his arm tighten.

I'm not in love with him, she thought frantically. Just grateful, that's all.

Alongside the boat wooded slopes had given way with dramatic suddenness to gaunt grey cliffs, rising vertically from the cold, deep water, slashed by waterfalls and echoing to the cries of gulls. Nicola fell silent, content to drink in the majestic work that tons of ice had wrought so long ago, and was indeed grateful that she was no longer held back by fear from enjoying this. When the boat bumped gently against a wharf by a primitive campsite at the far end of the fjord, and the captain said that anyone wanting to disembark and look around could be picked up by the next boat, she said eagerly, 'Let's Trent! We could climb part way up and get a great view of the water.'

He hesitated in a way she was to remember, glancing up at the sky where the clouds were now purple-edged. 'It might rain. We'd get wet.'

The air was very still, a heat wave shimmering over the water. 'It wouldn't matter if we did,' Nicola said gaily. 'We'd be dry in no time.' She laughed up at him, fluttering her lashes in a parody of one of her sisters.

He smiled reluctantly and led the way to the gang-plank, where two other passengers had also disembarked. As soon as Nicola's sneaker touched the ground the mosquitoes descended on her, whining, voracious mosquitoes that made her hurriedly roll her sleeves to her wrists and button her collar.

'Want to change your mind?' Trent asked.

But she was listening to one of the campers, a young man who would have been good-looking had his face not been swollen with bites, and whose advice was to climb up the gorge, above the tree-line, in order to leave the insects behind. She led the way along the path he had pointed out, swatting at her ear and then squashing a mosquito anchored on the back of her hand. It left a bright red patch of blood on her skin. 'Yuck,' she said.

Behind them the boat's engine growled into life. 'Too late now,' said Trent.

The path led through birch and alders where tiny yellow warblers flitted and sang, and where a pleasant scent of wood-smoke from the campfires hung in the air. From overhead, in counterpoint to the engine, came the distant growl of thunder. Nicola ignored it, her twin objectives being to climb high enough to see the waters of the fjord and also to leave the mosquitoes behind. And very soon the path claimed all her attention, for it deteriorated rapidly into heaps of rough-hewn granite boulders alternating with angled slopes of loose, slippery rock in which her sneakers had to scrabble for purchase. She soon stopped to catch her breath, her shirt sticking to her back, and said breathlessly to her companion, 'Not as many mosquitoes, are there?'

'You're an optimist, Nicola—there's one on your neck. Hold still.'

Nicola obeyed, tingling with awareness as Trent's fingers brushed her flesh. As though nature herself was in sympathy with her, a flash of lightning flickered in the still air, followed moments later by the grumble of thunder, much closer than last time. Trent's hand jerked against her neck; she winced at the tug on her hair.

'Sorry,' he said.

She glanced at him, puzzled. Because she was above him on the slope, his face was level with hers. The blue of his eyes was very dark, turned inwards, and there was tension in the line of his jaw and the set of his shoulders. 'Are you OK?' she said uncertainly.

'Out of condition,' he replied, not meeting her eyes. 'Are we going higher?'

'Sure . . . we've got lots of time. And a thunderstorm up here would be worth seeing, wouldn't it? You will be glad to know that, although afraid of water, boats and men, I love thunder and lightning.'

Trent did not laugh. In fact, Nicola was not even sure he had heard her. She turned away, convinced she would never in a hundred years be able to anticipate his responses, and began to climb again. Her muscles stretched to the challenge, and although the air was still oppressively hot they soon left behind both the trees and the mosquitoes. The sky had darkened; the next flash of lightning lit the cliff face with theatrical brilliance, and the thunder clapped like a huge burst of applause that echoed and re-echoed down the fjord.

Nicola sat down on the nearest hunk of granite and gazed out over the fjord. The water had taken on the purple tones of the sky, while the shadowed cliffs seemed to have hunched closer together. A flock of gulls, perhaps disturbed by the thunder, rose and fell like specks of shredded paper scattered to the wind. The boat was already out of sight. She and Trent could have been alone in the world.

Lightning flashed again, so close Nicola could see its bright, tangled roots seeking the earth; the thunder resonated through her body and shouted among the cliffs. She laughed out loud, exulting in the wildness and sheer energy of the storm, and saw, over the flatness of the plateau at the top of the cliffs, the dense grey cloud of approaching rain.

'We're going to get soaked!' she yelled, and laughed down at Trent.

He was standing below her, his back to her. His hands were thrust in his pockets, his shoulders a rigid line. Her laughter died in her throat. She said urgently, 'Trent—what's wrong?'

He shook his head, not looking at her. 'Nothing.'

In one short word she sensed an immense effort at control. She scrambled off the rock, her feet slithering in the shale, and touched his arm; it too was rigid, like a bar of steel. As she looked up into his face a brilliant flash of lightning split the sky, the crash of thunder inseparable from it, wrapping them both in noise: deafening, tangible noise. Trent's face convulsed, and Nicola felt the muscles under her fingertips shudder as though he had been struck with a whip. Yet even then he did not quite lose his formidable self-control.

Nicola took him by the arms, curving her warm fingers around his taut flesh. 'Trent, look at me—please!'

Another searing bolt of lightning was reflected in the dark pools of his eyes, and then the thunder enveloped them in its infernal music. He flinched, his features a rictus of pain and terrible fear, and Nicola flung herself against his body, holding him with all her strength, giving him the only comfort she could.

With the next flash of light he broke, clutching her to him as though she were the only person in the world who could save him. He was shivering violently, from a terror she could only imagine; she knew about such fear, and into her mind fell the image of a small girl clutching the keel of a boat in the windswept ocean. She held him as tightly as she could, rubbing the tense muscles of his back, murmuring over and over again, 'It's all right, Trent—I'm here. I won't leave you . . .'

A lurid streak of light, a crack of thunder like a cannon shot, and then the rain started. It lashed their faces and plastered their clothes to their bodies, blinding them, blanking out the cliffs and the fjord in a solid curtain of grey.

Nicola rubbed her eyes with one hand, raindrops running down her face like a thousand tears. If she were writing this scene, she thought crazily, she would do it differently. She would have a pine tree or a convenient cave for shelter. For here there was nothing; they were totally exposed. She tugged Trent down to crouch beside her among the rocks, awkwardly keeping her arms around him. Speech was impossible, for the rain was drumming on the boulders and her mouth filled with water if she opened it.

The next bolt of lightning was dimmer, the thunder lagging behind it. Soaked to the skin, rocking Trent's body in her arms, Nicola waited. Her ankle was bent under her. Her nose itched. No heroine worthy of her salt would be worrying about her nose, she thought with a desperate kind of humour, and wondered what on earth she was going to say to Trent.

The thunder grumbled in the distance, and the rain lessened. Her ankle sent shafts of pain up her leg. She said, 'Trent, I've got to move or I'm going to be permanently crippled and you'll have to carry me back to the boat.'

His head was bent; he said nothing. Nicola shifted her position, said, 'Ouch!' loudly, and felt pins and needles prickle her ankle. Then she reached over with one wet hand, raised Trent's chin and looked him full in the face. Her brown eyes very serious, she said matter-of-factly, 'I know what your demon is now, the black bird you said sat on your shoulder—you're terrified of thunder and lightning.' She had thought of saying frightened. But frightened was too weak a word to describe the animal-like convulsions that had racked his body, and this seemed a time for truth.

Trent said nothing. She added, 'As terrified as I was of the water and of boats. And, I would suspect, with as good a reason.'

Still he did not respond; he was avoiding her eyes. 'Say something!' she ordered in a fierce spurt of energy. 'But don't try and deny what happened.'

His head jerked up, deep lines scoring his face. 'What do you want me to say?' he blazed. 'That I'm a coward? That I'm a grown man who's scared out of his wits by a few claps of thunder and a bit of lightning? Is that what you want me to say?'

'It's a start. And with me of all people you surely shouldn't be ashamed.'

'Of course I am! Men are supposed to be the strong ones, not afraid of anything. Or if they are afraid, they're supposed to hide it. For God's sake, Nicola, I'm the one who should have been protecting you—not the other way round.'

'Why don't we forget what you're supposed to be and talk about what you are. *Why* are you so afraid of thunder, Trent?'

'Oh, hell, that's easy—from the time I was five my grandmother used to lock me up in the root cellar every time there was a thunderstorm. Dirt floor, stone walls, spiders and mice. No windows, but enough cracks in the door that I could see everything in each bolt of lightning before the darkness took over again, so thick I could taste it.'

Carefully keeping any expression out of her voice, Nicola asked, 'Why would she do that?'

'Because she hated me,' he said without a trace of emotion. 'From the moment I was born, she hated me.'

He was gazing at his hands, linked around his knees. Sitting very still, Nicola waited. 'My mother was her daughter,' he went on in a strained voice, 'and a rich woman in her own right. She fell madly in love with my father, eloped with him and went to Copenhagen to live with him. According to my grandmother, he married her for her money, and then broke her heart with the affairs he had with other women. At any rate, my mother died soon after I was born—my grandmother always said I killed her. So of course she hated me. Once the will was settled, my father vanished and I went to live with my grandmother; she was my closest relative.'

He seemed to have run out of words. Nicola said quietly, 'So she did things like lock you up during thunderstorms to make a man of you.'

'I look like my father. That made it worse.'

'She was wicked to punish you for things you couldn't possibly help! *You* weren't responsible for your mother's death any more than you can help the way you look.'

He gave her a faint smile. 'As an adult, I can only agree with you. As a small boy, I saw it differently.'

Nicola said forcefully, 'If you came out of all that only scared of thunderstorms, you're pretty well off.'

'I'm thirty-one years old and I've never married.'

I would marry you, she thought. The words were as unexpected as a bolt of lightning, and echoed in her mind as the thunder had reverberated among the cliffs.

'What's the matter?' Trent rapped.

Nicola looked at him, wide-eyed, and said, 'The woman who marries you will be a very fortunate woman.'

It was plainly not what he had expected. His smile suddenly genuine, he said, 'You're a sweetheart, Nicola.'

But not yours?

Perhaps the question showed in her face. With a rough exclamation Trent put his arms around her and kissed her, an awkward, intense kiss of devastating honesty. Then he pushed her away. 'I won't fall in love with you,' he said harshly. 'It wouldn't be fair to you.'

'Why not?' she whispered.

'Because I'll never marry. For obvious reasons.'

Her tongue tripping over the words, she said, 'Then I'll also state the obvious. You're not your father and I'm not your mother, Trent. We're two different people. And your grandmother was a wicked woman.'

He reached over and ruffled her wet hair. 'You look very sweet when you're angry.'

'Don't patronise me!'

He met her anger with an anger of his own. 'All right, I won't. But don't go building castles in the air around me—I won't play.'

'No! You'll just kiss me whenever it suits you, string me a line about seduction, and then push me aside.'

'I should never had kissed you at all. You've been hurt twice already—how can I hurt you again?'

'You already have,' she said quietly.

'Don't, Nicola—please don't!'

The pain in his voice gave her the strength to say, with a touch of desperation, 'Trent, you're cutting yourself off from love and intimacy—from all that makes life worth living.'

'I've never allowed myself to love a woman.'

'You could start with me.'

His face set, he said, 'There's an hour before the next boat. Do you want to go back to the wharf?'

Nicola got to her feet in one swift movement, feeling as though she had been rejected from a magical place before having the chance to see what made it so magical, let alone to enjoy it. And this time it had nothing to do with her sisters.

'I'm going to climb higher,' she said.

'I'll wait here. Be careful.'

She turned her back and began scaling the wet rocks with ferocious energy; and not until she was sure she was out of Trent's sight did she stop. Her breath was rasping in her throat, and her damp clothes clung uncomfortably to her body. Perching herself on the flat top of a boulder, she cupped her chin in her hands and gazed out over the landscape.

The view was magnificent. Through a gap in the clouds a shaft of sunlight illuminated the shining black flanks of the cliffs and the sleek surface of the fjord. The rain had stopped; silence, the silence of millennia, beat against Nicola's ears. She felt small, and insignificant, and very much alone.

She thought of Maryanne and Flint, whose estrangement could end if they were marooned in a thunderstorm in the mountains near a convenient cave, and wondered if she would have the heart to write the scene.

She could not rewrite the one that had just occurred. Trent would not, to use his own word, play.

Trent would not be hero to her heroine.

At dinner time that evening Nicola arrived at the front steps of the main house the same time as Suzie. Suzie, as usual, looked effortlessly beautiful, a filmy skirt rippling about her calves, her long black hair loose on her shoulders. Nicola, who had had a silent trip back from the fjord with Trent and had not seen him since, was feeling tired and dispirited. This had not stopped her from putting on a stylish purple shirt and gold hooped earrings with her cotton trousers. She straightened her spine, produced a creditable smile and said, 'Hello, Suzie.'

Suzie smiled back; she always reminded Nicola of a well-fed cat when she smiled. 'Did you enjoy the outing with Trent?'

Into Nicola's mind dropped the image of Trent shuddering in her arms. Heroes, she thought confusedly, are not afraid of thunderstorms. Flint would not be. Flint wasn't afraid of anything. So did that mean Trent was not a hero? Was he a real man instead, one who had shared long-held, unbearable memories with her and thereby given her part of himself? He had run from her afterwards, but perhaps that was to be expected. She said soberly, 'Some of it, I did.'

Suzie widened her eyes with mock innocence. 'You don't sound very enthusiastic . . . didn't he come across?'

'Oh, shush!' said Nicola.

'That's not much of an answer.'

'It's all the answer you're going to get.'

'You've changed,' Suzie said, giving Nicola a frank appraisal, the kind she would only have given an equal. 'You're not nearly the little mouse you were when you arrived. But I'm still not convinced you can handle Trent—he's too much man for you.'

Everything in Suzie's bearing implied a superior knowledge of the man they were discussing. Nicola subdued a hot pang of jealousy and said sweetly, 'We'll just have to see, won't we?'

Suzie laughed. 'You can come to my party on Saturday night if you want to,' she said generously. 'Daniel and

I are giving it.' She smiled again, a lazy, satiated smile.
'Bring Trent if you like...oh, there's Daniel.'

Without waiting for a reply to her invitation, which
was just as well because Nicola had no idea what to say,
she ran gracefully down the steps and across the lawn,
her hair and her skirt flying out behind her, and threw
herself into Daniel's arms. They kissed with an explic-
itness that made Nicola look away; she hurried up the
steps and into the cool, high-ceilinged hall.

The invitation was an accolade, she thought drily, and
had very little to do with her brave purple shirt. For the
changes in herself were inner changes, to do with confidence because she had conquered her worst fear, and
pride because she was freeing her emotions. She knew,
in her heart, that Trent wanted her. His body, his kisses,
his words, had all given her that message; and it was a
message she had to trust.

She heard Suzie's rippling laugh from outside, and
hurried into the dining-room.

The next day it rained, a steady downpour that drummed
on the roof of the cabin and gurgled in the gutters. Nicola
got Flint and Maryanne into the cave and there discovered that they were not prepared to mend their dif-
ferences. Although part of her was disconcerted, because
she had had the scene so neatly wrapped up in her mind,
another part rather enjoyed the independent life her
characters had taken on, and was interested to see where
it would lead. She worked hard all day, and was editing
the day's work at nine-thirty that evening when a knock
came on her door. 'Come in,' she called, and for some
reason was convinced Suzie would drift in the door.

Trent came in and stood by the door, his yellow rain
slicker dripping on the mat. He pushed back the hood,

his eyes very blue in the lamplight. 'Still working?' he said in a neutral voice.

'Yes,' said Nicola inanely, standing up. Her hair was untidy, because she was in the habit of running her fingers through it whenever her plot got mired down, and there was a pencil stuck behind her ear because despite the computer she still had to scribble things down. She was bare-footed; her jeans had shrunk in Olivia's dryer; her T-shirt had two rather magnificent tigers across her breasts over a caption that said 'Extinction is Forever', and she was not wearing a bra. She added, even more inanely, 'How are you?'

'Fine.'

And there the conversation stopped. Nicola found herself drinking in every detail of Trent's appearance, from his broad shoulders in the bulky jacket to his long legs encased in rain-spattered jeans, and was wholly delighted that it was he and not Suzie. Her eyes dancing, she said, 'Take off your——'

'When you look at me like that, all I want to do is make love to you,' he interrupted hoarsely.

Nicola raised her chin, knowing she was blushing, and said spiritedly, 'You'd have to kiss me first, and you swore off that.'

His smile was crooked. 'I could make love to you without kissing you.'

Her breath caught in her throat; under the tiger's striped flanks her nipples hardened involuntarily. She saw his eyes drop, and clutched the back of her chair, biting her lip. 'Is that why you came here?' she asked in a voice that shook in spite of herself. 'To make love to me?'

He said harshly, 'I came to tell you I'll be away for the next ten days—I knew you'd wonder if you couldn't hear any sounds from next door.'

'But you'll be back?' she blurted.

'Yes. But Nicola, I warned you—don't expect anything of me.'

She remembered the grandmother who had hated him from birth, and said gently, 'I expect honesty. Which you're giving me. It was kind of you to come and tell me.'

He let out his breath in a jagged sigh. 'The long-range weather reports say rain for the next week. So Olivia wants me to join up with a logging crew forty miles from here and cut her winter's supply of wood.'

'A change from making turkeys,' Nicola said with a deadpan expression on her face.

'Eagles, Nicola.'

Some of the tension had left his face. She said lightly, 'Hot chocolate before you turn in?'

He hesitated. She added, looking at him through her lashes, 'I promise not to rape you.'

'You couldn't—because I'd be willing,' he drawled, and watched the colour rise in her cheeks. 'Sure, I'll stay.'

Wishing the hotplate and tiny refrigerator were anywhere but in the living-room, Nicola busied herself with mugs and milk. She made a rich, frothy hot chocolate with marshmallows and flakes of dark chocolate floating on top, and passed one of the mugs to Trent. 'Cheers,' she said, raising her own and then taking a big gulp.

'It tastes great,' Trent said. 'We used to get hot chocolate at boarding-school, but it was nothing like this.'

She drew him out to talk more about his childhood; as if his initial story of the root cellar and the thunderstorms had freed him, he spoke matter-of-factly about other deprivations, deprivations he seemed to take for granted. Nicola kept her compassion and anger well hidden, although her heart ached for him, and every now and then interjected some of the funnier stories of what it had been like growing up with two beautiful sisters. 'They were very good when Gran was dying, though,' she said fairly. 'They both live in Halifax, but they visited as often as they could...it was while I stayed with Gran that I got interested in writing. I used to write short stories for her, sketches of some of the neighbours and the fishermen we knew. They used to make her laugh—although I'd have been sued for libel if they'd ever gone to print.'

'After my grandmother—whom I cannot imagine calling Gran—had her first heart attack, I tried to visit her. But she wouldn't see me...never forgave me, I suppose. I've come to terms with that. And with her will. She left me fifty dollars out of a fortune of several hundred thousand.'

'You could have contested it,' Nicola said hotly.

'I went out and made my own money instead.'

'And how did you do that, Trent?' she asked demurely.

'I'm an architect.' He glanced at his watch. 'Good lord, it's nearly midnight,' he exclaimed. 'I've got to leave in six hours, and I'm not packed.' He stood up, holding out the empty mug. 'Thanks, Nicola.'

Nicola had been perched on her chair, her bare feet tucked underneath her, for she had not quite trusted herself to share the chesterfield with him. She would not see him for ten days, she thought painfully, realising how much she took for granted the small noises of his presence next door, and stood up as well. One foot had gone to sleep. She staggered a little just as he stepped forward and handed her the mug. His work boot, steel-toed, landed on her instep.

She dropped the mug, yelped with pain and clutched her foot in both hands. The mug bounced on the floor and miraculously did not break. 'Nicola, I'm sorry!'

Trent exclaimed. 'Here, sit down and let me see your foot.'

Off balance, she fell back into the chair. 'It's nothing,' she mumbled. 'You startled me, that's all.'

But he had circled her ankle in one hand, stroking her blue-veined instep where a red abrasion marred the skin. Her foot was fine-boned, lost in his much larger hand; with an incoherent exclamation he put his arms around her and held her tightly to his chest. 'You know I want you,' he muttered against her hair. 'How can I pretend I don't?'

Her voice muffled by his shirt, knowing the words for the truth, Nicola said, 'I want you, too.'

Kneeling by the chair, he pushed her a little away from him. 'I've never gone from woman to woman—perhaps because that's what my father did. So this could just be a simple case of deprivation.'

'Except you didn't take Suzie to bed.'

'No, I didn't take Suzie to bed. So I guess it's more than deprivation, huh?'

Knowing she believed him, Nicola still had to ask the obvious. 'Whyever didn't you?'

'Not my type,' he said with a touch of flippancy. But then his voice deepened. 'I like honesty and courage and brown eyes that melt my heart.'

'Oh, Trent,' she said helplessly, very near tears.

Abruptly he stood up, his boots scraping on the floor. 'I've got to get out of here, Nicola—I still mean what I said on the mountain.'

She stayed where she was, not at all sure that her knees would hold her up. Searching for the right thing to say, knowing he was worth fighting for with every ounce of the courage and honesty he admired in her, she met his eyes and said quietly, 'I'll be here when you get back.'

Making no attempt to touch him, she added with a warm, unforced smile, 'Don't let any trees fall on you, will you?'

His face was so full of strain that it took all her willpower not to throw herself in his arms. He said tightly, 'I won't. And you remember you're not quite ready to swim across the bay yet.'

Their words were like a hedge, she thought, hiding and yet not hiding what they meant. 'I promise.'

As if the words were being dragged from him, he said, 'When I get back, we could take a day off and climb Gros Morne.'

Gros Morne was a mountain ten miles from the fjord. 'I'd love to,' Nicola said, her lips curving with delight.

'You're so beautiful when you smile like that,' he muttered. 'Goodnight, Nicola.'

From the chair she watched him stride across the room and go out into the darkness. And for a long time she stayed in the chair, listening to the sounds he made as he packed and showered. Only when the rooms next door had been silent for over half an hour did she quietly get ready for bed.

CHAPTER EIGHT

TRENT had been gone for nine days. During his absence Olivia's lawns had grown shaggy and the delphiniums had bloomed. Every time Nicola saw the tall purple and blue stalks she thought of Trent; she thought of him quite frequently when she was nowhere near the perennial garden, too. She wondered how he was. She remembered all he had told her about his grandmother and the loveless house he had grown up in. She missed him acutely. And she sublimated as much of this emotion as she could in the passionate peregrinations of Maryanne and Flint.

The pile of manuscript in her drawer was steadily growing. Nicola knew the story was good, that it was carried along on its own energy and that the emotions rang true. Olivia, who had connections almost everywhere, knew an agent in Toronto, and had already promised her the manuscript by the end of the summer, so Nicola worked as many as ten hours a day, because an acceptance would make the rest of her university degree a certainty.

She went to bed about ten the evening of the ninth day, holding to the excitement that she would see Trent tomorrow, and fell asleep immediately. It was pitch dark when she woke. She lay very still, her heart racing, her ears straining for the noise that had woken her. Then it came again. A floorboard creaking next door, a small thud as if something had been dropped.

Trent wasn't due home until tomorrow. Who was it?

The sounds were furtive, stealthy, as though the person, whoever it was, was trying very hard to be quiet.

It could be Trent, come back early. Or it could be a thief, after his computer and the Piaget watch.

If it was Trent, all she had to do was call out. If it was not, she was a long way from the main house.

Then Nicola heard the small, homely sounds of the tap running and of someone brushing his teeth. It had to be Trent, she thought in a rush of relief. No thief that she had ever heard of had stopped in mid-burglary to clean his teeth. 'Trent?' she called out in a carrying voice. 'Is that you?'

The water stopped. 'Yeah,' came Trent's deep voice. 'Sorry, Nicola, I didn't mean to wake you. I was trying to be quiet.'

'Can I come and say hello?'

The words had come out on their own volition. She gulped inwardly and waited for his reply. After a pause she measured in seconds, he said, 'Sure—just for a minute.'

It was not the most reassuring of replies. She got out of bed, switched on the light and quickly dressed in jeans and a bulky sweater. After dashing cold water on her face and running a brush through her hair—which was now curling round her ears—she hurried over to Trent's side of the cabin.

He came out of the bathroom as she closed the door behind her, and for a moment she thought she was in the wrong place. The beginnings of a beard covered the lower part of his face, a rough reddish-blond beard, changing him into a stranger. He was wearing a red and black checked wool shirt, mud-stained jeans and heavy wool socks; his eyes were dark-circled.

Any daydreams Nicola might have had about throwing herself into his arms died stillborn, for there was something guarded and watchful in his face that made it impossible. So she stated the obvious instead. 'You look tired.'

'We worked from dawn to dusk, and then the serious business of the day began—poker.' He ran a hand over his jaw. 'I don't think I want to see another pack of cards for as long as I live. Or a bottle of rum.'

He was avoiding her eyes. She said flatly, 'I'm glad you're back.'

'A hot shower's going to feel pretty good.' He gave an exaggerated yawn.

She should not have come. Suppressing a disappointment so keen that it was like a physical pain, Nicola mumbled, 'Well, goodnight,' and turned away, her vision blurred by tears.

Her hand was on the door when he said urgently, 'Nicola——'

She pulled the door open, her head bent, too proud to want him to know she was crying. 'I'll see you tomorrow,' she said.

A hand fell on her shoulder; his socked feet had been silent on the floor. She jumped and said fiercely, 'I'm going!'

He pulled her round to face him, saw the sheen of tears over her eyes and said hoarsely, 'God, I missed you—I thought about you day and night, I wanted you in my bed, and now that you're here in front of me the smartest thing I could do would be to start running and not stop until I hit Vancouver.'

Her tears were forgotten. 'So is that what you're going to do?' she demanded. 'Because I missed you too, Trent.'

'You tear me apart,' he said in a low voice.

There was so much pain in his face that Nicola's anger died. And he had said that he had missed her: an admission that warmed her heart, for it spoke of emotion, and emotion was what Trent feared. Instinctively she reached up her hand and laid it on his cheek. 'You're exhausted,' she said gently. 'Have a shower and go to bed—tomorrow, as Gran used to say, is another day.'

As she let her hand fall to her side, she could see him making an immense effort to speak normally. 'I'll have to spend two or three days cleaning up the lawns and the flowerbeds. The first fine day after that, we could climb the mountain . . . you look tired too, Nicola.'

'I've been working hard. But each day I've gone for a swim in the bay with Karen.'

His smile was almost natural. 'Good for you! The noise of the shower won't keep you awake?'

'I'll be fine. 'Night.' She flashed a smile at him and slipped out of the door. Nor did the shower keep her awake. It was the unappeased longing to be holding Trent in her arms that kept Nicola staring into the darkness long after the rooms next door had fallen silent.

Trent and Nicola set off in the truck to drive to Gros Morne early one crisp August morning a week after Trent had come back. Each had a haversack with a picnic lunch and juice; assuming there would be mosquitoes, Nicola had dressed in long trousers and a long-sleeved cotton shirt. The sky was a vivid blue patched with fluffy little clouds so white they looked newly washed; she did not think there would be any thunderstorms today.

They could see the mountain from the road, a long grey hump of a mountain, rising like the back of a whale from a sea of green. 'It's an hour-and-a-half hike to the base,' Trent said casually. 'Then a couple of hours to get to the top.' He grinned at her. 'Depending what sort of shape you're in.'

'I'm going to make my excuses early,' she responded pertly. 'I've spent far too much time this summer sitting in front of a computer.'

He parked the truck in the shade of a tree and climbed out with long-limbed grace. 'The trail begins over there.'

Keep your mind on the trail, Nicola scolded herself, and adjusted her haversack comfortably on her back. They wound through the trees for the first half-hour, then emerged into the open, in knee-high brush, the hills rising all around them under a wide expanse of sky. It was hot, without a breath of a breeze, and by the time Nicola had crossed the little creek at the base of the mountain her shirt was sticking to her back under her pack and her hair clinging damply to her neck.

Trent was gazing at the gorge that snaked up the side of the mountain. They had been walking in single file, and he had spoken very little on the way in; they had not had, Nicola thought, what she would call a real conversation ever since that brief, intense and totally inconclusive conversation a week ago in his cabin in the middle of the night. Right now he did not look like a man torn apart by emotion. His emotions looked well under control. Or non-existent.

Perhaps he had only brought her here because he had said he would, and whatever his faults he was a man of his word.

'Ready?' he asked briefly.

The slope did not look very steep from here. Nicola nodded.

Twenty-five minutes later she decided appearances could indeed be deceptive, for she was looking straight up at a nearly vertical climb among jagged heaps of granite. There were no trees on Gros Morne, and the sun beat down on the rocks. Trent was already well ahead of her, and appeared to have no interest in whether she was following him or not. Resolutely she began to climb. To think that this outing had sounded romantic when Trent had first suggested it!

Trent was waiting for her part way up the gorge, but only to point out to her in the distance the blue strip of water that was Bonne Bay and behind it the red rocks of the ancient plateau called the Tableland, still patched with snow. Gasping for breath, Nicola put down her haversack and took a long drink of juice, wishing she had worn her shorts, wishing Trent would sweep her off her feet as Flint had swept Maryanne five pages ago, wishing they were at the top. She could not see the top. Maybe it didn't exist.

Trent, who had spent nine days hauling logs around in the woods, was hardly out of breath. Nicola said with an excusable touch of irony, 'You go first,' and put the juice bottle back in her pack.

'Sure you're going to make it?'

'I'll get there if it kills me,' she vowed, thoroughly disliking the glint of mockery in his eye.

She toiled upwards. Two groups of hikers passed her, calling out cheerful greetings. Sweat dripped into her eyes and trickled down between her breasts, while inside her sneakers her feet were burningly hot. One of the disadvantages of being a writer with a self-imposed deadline was the dearth of physical exercise, she thought, wiping her forehead with the back of her hand and squinting upwards to where the trail vanished on the skyline. That might be the top. Or it might, when she got there, simply reveal another slope to be climbed.

But it was the top. A gentle rise covered with fragrant junipers and crowberry stretched out in front of her. Lying full-length on the ground was Trent, his head pillowed on his pack, his big body perfectly relaxed. 'I've been waiting for you for ages,' he murmured.

Conquering a strong urge to kick him, Nicola plunked herself down beside him and hauled off her sneakers and socks, wiggling her toes in ecstatic relief. 'The only nice thing about that climb is that it's over,' she said darkly, and began to unpack her lunch.

Egg sandwiches and carrot sticks eaten in front of a sweeping panorama of craggy, green-clad hills and azure sea made Nicola feel much better. She and Trent started to talk about books they had read and movies they had seen; safe, impersonal topics that somehow emboldened her to say into a pause in the conversation, 'I was beginning to think you didn't want me here today.'

He was leaning on one elbow peeling an apple. He looked up, the knife still. 'I want you here, all right. Too much.'

She grimaced. 'You have a funny way of showing it.'

He carefully removed an elaborate coil of peel. 'No practice.'

'Trent Livingstone,' she said strongly, 'you are quite the most gorgeous man I have ever laid eyes on! Don't you dare tell me the women aren't falling all over you.'

'If they're falling, it's because I'm not there to catch them.' He circled the stem with the blade and pulled it out. As she gave an exasperated sigh, he went on, 'Nicola, I've spent time in the company of women, I've had affairs with women—sophisticated women who wouldn't think of standing with their hands on their hips yelling at me like you do.' He cut a slice of apple, balancing it on the knife blade. 'I've never let one past my defences, though. Never. Until you came along. With that keep-your-distance look in your big brown eyes. With your terror of the water and your temper and your gentleness. You scare the hell out of me. Much easier to climb ten mountains.' He took a bite of the apple and began to chew.

Nicola, temporarily struck dumb, gaped at him. When it became obvious he had had his say, she snorted, 'And that's all?'

'Yes,' he replied with underlying savagery. 'I'm not going to haul you down into the shrubbery to make love and I'm not going to say I need you.' Leaning over to lace his boots, he added irritably, 'Let's get moving.'

The temper he had mentioned very much in evidence, Nicola snapped, 'You sure believe in control, don't you?'

'How else do you think I survived my grandmother?' he snarled, swung his pack on his back and strode off towards the cairns that marked the trail across the plateau. Nicola reached for her sneakers. For the first seven years of her life she had been surrounded by love and security, and she had been building on that foundation ever since. But Trent had had no such foundation, and in consequence was afraid of love. If he had opted for control instead, she could scarcely blame him.

She stood up and started off after him; but he was walking too fast for her to close the gap between them.

There was a light wind wafting over the top of Gros Morne. Tiny circlets of Arctic flowers clung to the scanty pockets of earth, and families of rock ptarmigan were clucking among the tumbled rocks. The green hills basked under the sun. Nicola tramped along, her eyes straying towards Trent's tall figure more often than she liked. She had better be very careful as far as Trent Livingstone was concerned. She certainly roused strong emotions in him; but he had no intention of allowing himself to fall in love with her.

On the far side of the plateau a steep path wound down the side of the mountain. The wind died instantly. The hills quivered in the heat. Nicola had drunk all her juice and eaten her apple; her throat parched and her feet feeling like live coals in her sneakers, she put one foot in front of the other with grim determination and vowed that she would not complain even if Trent stopped long enough to give her the chance. Next time he suggested an outing, she would tell him where he could go. Flint in his very worst moods had nothing on Trent.

The trail was skirting a valley, the stream dammed into a series of ponds by beavers. Nicola watched them for a while. Then the path descended further to a small lake with a sandy shore edged by alder bushes. She dipped her fingers in. The water felt deliciously cool.

She glanced around. No one in sight, and she was fairly sure no one had been close behind her on the descent. Ducking into the alders, she stripped off her shirt and trousers, leaving them in a pile on the ground. She had put a light cotton T-shirt in her pack; putting it on, she edged clear of the bushes. Still no one. In her underwear and the shirt she slipped into the water and began to swim.

She had never in her life felt anything as refreshing as that lake water as it slid smoothly over her body, easing the tension between her shoulders and laving her sore feet. She dived beneath the surface, opening her eyes as Trent had taught her, then surfaced, her hair streaming water into her face. Laughing to herself in sheer pleasure, she swam towards the opposite shore, ducking under again and taking several long strokes under the water. She shouldn't be angry with Trent. He had, after all, made this possible.

The water was colder at this end of the lake. She practised her backstroke, kicking up spray with her feet, then took a deep breath and slid under the water again. This time she swam until her lungs ached before she burst up into the air, her hair slicked to her skull.

'*Nicola!* My God . . . Nicola.'

Wiping the water from her eyes, Nicola looked over her shoulder. Trent was standing knee-deep in the lake, still in his jeans and shirt, his face so distraught that she said blankly, 'What's the matter?'

'Come here.'

It was not a tone of voice she had heard him use before; she had no idea what it signified. In swift short strokes she swam towards him, stopping a few feet away where the water was still deep. 'What's happened? You look awful.'

As he waded out so that the lake lapped his calves, Nicola touched bottom with her bare toes and stood up. Trent took two more long steps, caught her in his arms and crushed her to his body.

Through his shirt she could feel the hard pounding of his heart; he was holding her so tightly that she could hardly breathe. Wondering if he had gone mad, she gasped, 'Are you all right?'

'I was nearly at the base of the mountain when I realised I couldn't see you behind me. So I started back-tracking until I came to the lake. Then I saw your shirt and trousers on the ground . . . and nothing but an empty stretch of water.' He clutched her convulsively. 'God, Nicola, I think I died a thousand deaths in those few seconds before you surfaced.'

Nicola had a vivid imagination and could picture the scene all too clearly. 'I didn't drown . . . but I might suffocate if you don't let go.'

His grip loosened. But instead of releasing her, he swung her up into his arms and waded nearer to shore before letting her feet drop back in the water. One arm around her shoulders, the other clasping her waist, he began to kiss her, fierce, impassioned kisses that made her head whirl. And then she heard him mutter as he nibbled at the softness of her lips, 'I love you . . . Nicola, I love you.'

She *was* drowning. Or else she was dreaming. Shoving against his shirt with her palms, she croaked, '*What* did you say?'

His answer was to kiss her again, a long, deep kiss so explicit and so intense that words seemed redundant. Nicola had never been kissed like that before: as though the man's heart and soul was in his kiss, as though, flame-like, it held truth and love at its centre.

Shaken to the core, she clung to him, and heard him whisper against her throat, 'Sweetheart, I love you.'

He raised his head. His eyes, a burning blue, bored into her dazed brown ones. He said as slowly as though speaking to a child, 'I thought you had drowned. It was then that I realised how I've been running for the last three weeks—running from the knowledge that I'd fallen in love.' His smile was twisted. 'Something I vowed I'd never do. Certainly something I told you I'd never do.'

He let his lips travel the length of her neck, to linger in the hollow at its base. With one hand he cupped her breast, watching her eyes widen with startled pleasure as through the wet fabric of her shirt he teased the nipple to hardness. 'I want to make love to you,' he said huskily. 'I want to taste every inch of your body.'

From behind him, as though from another planet, Nicola heard a chorus of wolf whistles. 'Go for it, man!' a male voice yelled, and a girl's voice giggled, 'Ronnie, shut up.'

Although Trent was partially shielding her with his body, Nicola could see a group of hikers on the trail near the lake, teenagers by the look of them. One made the victory sign, another raised his hands in mock applause; the girls were tittering, the boys guffawing. Nicola said drily, 'Maybe we shouldn't make love right here.'

It was not the way she would have written the scene in her book, for Maryanne and Flint would have made wild and passionate love on the shores of the lake,

undisturbed by either human intruders or, more mun-
danely, mosquitoes.

The hikers vanished behind the alders. Trent looked
down at her, and suddenly they both began to laugh,
great whoops of laughter that destroyed any remnants
of passion. Said Nicola, 'I trust they didn't steal my
clothes. While we were otherwise engaged.'

'They did not. I think you'd better put them on. Fast.'

From the hill drifted other voices. Nicola said comically, 'This placc is like Times Square. I won't be long.'

She sloshed through the lake to the heap of clothing
by the bushes and stripped off her T-shirt. Then, as
though pulled by a force greater than herself, she turned
to face Trent; he was watching her intently, his body
with the frozen stillness of the buck who had sighted the
doe. Naked except for her briefs, the air caressing her
wet skin with warm fingers, Nicola gazed across the
stretch of water and with a strange sense of destiny knew
she belonged to this man.

It was not how she had always pictured love; it seemed
to have nothing to do with love, being both more
instinctive and more elemental than any romantic
fantasies she had ever harboured. But fate had brought
her to this moment of meeting Trent on the shores of a
wilderness lake; her body had been fashioned as the mate
to his.

Feeling as though a lifetime had been compressed into
a few seconds, Nicola picked up her shirt and jeans and
pulled them on, making no attempt to dry herself. Then
she sat down to do up her sneakers. Trent was lacing his
boots on the shore; she watched him for a moment,
hearing his words echo in her mind. I love you, he had
said. I love you.

She had not, in response, said those same words to
him. Still did not feel ready to say them.

Did she love him? As logic usurped that profound sense of belonging, she could recognise how fiercely she desired him, and how little he resembled either Allan or George. But what if Cheryl or Gayle showed up? Would Trent be faithful to her? Or would he be drawn into the orbit of her sisters, bewitched from her side as first George, and then Allan had been?

So am I afraid to love Trent? she wondered, tying her laces in an elaborate bow. Afraid to trust in a happy ending?

'Ready, Nicola?' Trent called.

Quickly she laced her other sneaker and swung her haversack on her back. It was much lighter and her feet felt wonderful. Shaking off both logic and emotion, she got back on the trail, grinned at him impudently, and said, 'Hi, handsome.'

'Careful,' he said. 'We could always make love in that raspberry patch.'

'You're not that handsome,' she said primly, and headed down the trail. She felt very happy. But was that love?

In single file, followed fairly closely by a family with three children, they walked to the base of the mountain and then back to the truck. With some difficulty, because every leg muscle she owned was sore, Nicola climbed up into the seat. 'Remind me to get more details next time you ask me out for a hike,' she grumbled.

Trent reached behind the seat and produced two frosted bottles of beer from a small cooler. Holding them just out of reach, he said, 'Repeat after me—I had a wonderful time.'

'Not only handsome—practical, too.' She fluttered her lashes. 'Can you cook?'

'I can burn bannock over a camp fire as well as the next man,' he said, passing her a beer then tilting the other bottle to his lips and taking three or four deep swallows.

Nicola watched the muscles move in his throat and wondered what would have happened at the side of the lake if the crowd of teenagers had not appeared. Trent said thickly, 'We can't make love in the truck, either, Nicola.'

She flushed scarlet. Still holding his beer, his other hand lying along the back of the seat, Trent leaned forward and kissed her very deliberately, his lips lingering until Nicola ached with a hunger so primitive and so immediate that she felt she was discovering herself for the first time. Then he drew back, adding with a calmness belied by the hammering pulse at the base of his throat, 'Although I'm not sure I want to wait much longer...shall we go back?'

She nodded, quite unable to speak, and discovered she was no longer the slightest bit interested in the beer. Fastening her seat belt, she sat quietly as they drove to the Eyrie, but the ache of hunger did not subside, and when they had walked through the pine grove to the clearing in front of the cabin it was still with her. She stopped at a point halfway between her steps and Trent's, and waited.

He said, standing a careful distance away from her, 'Nicola, I want to make love to you.'

She understood completely. The choice was hers: neither with lips nor hands would he coerce her. She said with absolute honesty, the colour rising in her cheeks again, 'I've never made love with anyone before, Trent. So I'm not protected against a pregnancy, either.'

In the book she was writing, she thought wildly, such pragmatic but all-important details would never surface. Maryanne would have fallen into Flint's arms without a thought for the consequences. But this was the real world. And in the real world of here and now, those consequences could be wrong for both herself and Trent.

He said incredulously, 'But you were engaged to Allan.'

'Only for two days. Then Cheryl arrived.' Her face full of all the old doubts, Nicola gazed up at him.

'I swear I would never leave you for another woman,' Trent said forcefully. 'Not for your sisters, not for anyone else. It's *you* I want.' Then he quirked his brow, deliberately trying to lighten the atmosphere. 'Nor will I do anything to make you pregnant—having only just discovered that I love you, I'm not quite ready to add a baby to the scenario.'

'But——'

'Sweetheart, don't worry. What I want most of all is to hold you in my arms knowing that I love you.'

Feeling very much as though she were stepping into unknown waters, waters whose depths she had no inkling of, Nicola said lightly, 'Your place or mine?'

Although her eyes were very clear, her stance was full of tension. 'Mine,' he said, and, picking her up in his arms, he began to climb the steps. But at the top he added, laughter warming his voice, 'In the movies this always looks easy—but how am I supposed to open two separate doors without dropping you?'

The screen door opened outwards and the wooden door inwards. 'I'll open the doors and you hold on to me—it's called equality,' Nicola chuckled.

So when Trent strode across the living-room to the bedroom they were both laughing. He pushed the bedroom door open with his knee, bent down to put her on the bed, sat beside her and began unlacing his boots. He said calmly, 'The room should be full of red roses and I should have champagne on ice...sorry about that.'

'I like pink roses and beer,' said Nicola and kicked off her sneakers. She felt very frightened; Trent, so close to her on the bed, seemed like a stranger. 'I haven't said I love you,' she burst out.

'I noticed that.' He stretched out on the bed and pulled her down to lie at his side. 'How about third time lucky, Nicola?' He tweaked her hair. 'After all, you've only got two sisters.'

His breath was fanning her cheek. There were tiny dark specks in the blue of his irises and she could feel the weight of his thigh against her own. As her heart began to race in her breast, impulsively she put her arms around his neck and kissed him on the mouth. It was an awkward kiss, untutored and tentative; but it changed him from a stranger to Trent, whom she knew in some ways better than anyone else in the world.

Then Trent kissed her, another of those slow, devastatingly sensual kisses that seemed to melt every bone in her body. He had hooked his thigh around hers, drawing her so close to him that she could feel through his jeans all the hardness and power that was his need of her. Like a shirt she had casually dropped to the floor, her fear dropped from her. This was Trent. She belonged to him. She nibbled at his lower lip, burying her fingers in the silky thickness of his hair, then tracing the line of his ear, the ridge of his brows, the flat planes of his cheeks, as though she were blind and this was the only way she could learn what he was like.

Her fingertips moved as delicately as butterflies over his face; he lay still, his eyes intent on her. Nicola said with sudden intensity, 'Do you know something? I've never felt this close to a man before. Never.'

'This is only the beginning,' Trent said huskily.

One by one he undid the buttons on her shirt, pushing it back so that her ivory skin was bared to his gaze. Then he circled her breast with his lips, his fingers exploring the softly swelling flesh. Nicola, shivering inwardly from a pleasure so intense she wanted it never to end, slid one hand under his shirt and for the first time felt the warm, hard muscle bands of his chest and the tangle of his body hair.

Again their eyes met, his a piercing blue, hers deep pools that only wanted to draw him into their depths. He said, 'This is a new country for me too, Nicola. No barriers, no defences ... nothing keeping us apart, and only love bringing us together.'

'Trust, as well,' she said seriously.

'And the promise of joy.'

He drew her closer, moving against her so that her breasts abraded against his body hair, then cupping her flesh in his palms, and all the while he watched the sensations ripple across her face. She was hiding nothing, open to him, each sunburst of discovery a gift to him.

They undressed slowly, in a silence broken only by Nicola's tiny whimpers of delight and Trent's murmured endearments; like a film in slow motion they wound their naked limbs around each other, kissed and caressed each other, gave each other pleasure for pleasure.

More than once, lying in her own bed on the other side of the wall, Nicola had fantasised two naked bodies entwined in the act of love; she now was discovering how limited her fantasies had been. Nothing had prepared her for the burning compulsion of desire, or for Trent's exquisite patience in feeding that desire. He had tasted every inch of her breasts until she had thought she would faint from delight. But then he had drawn away to kiss her mouth, their tongues dancing, and with touching innocence she had begun her own exploration of the bone and muscle and sinew of this man who in some strange way belonged to her and on whom she

wanted to put her seal. The unexpected smoothness of
his skin. The taut belly and the hard arch of his pelvis.
The weight of his thigh. Each came with its shock of
surprise and wonderment, each added to her joy and to
her hunger.

Trent's hand, stroking the curve of her waist and hip,
drifted down her belly to seek out, between her legs, the
centre of that hunger. The pleasure, this time, was so
sharp as to be almost pain; swiftly it gathered into waves
like those of the sea, one after another, until Nicola was
writhing under his touch and moaning his name, lost to
everything but an ever-gathering need for completion.
Then she cried out, once, twice, her body arching into
his, her nails digging into his back, as she sank into sea
caves she had never known existed, dark, mysterious
places now shot through with brilliance.

When she opened her eyes again, she was still lying
on the bed and the evening sun was shining through the
window to cross Trent's body with light and shadow. 'I
travelled a long way,' she whispered, and suddenly,
fiercely, pulled him closer, knowing only that she wanted
to give him that same plummeting into darkness that
was the body's release; pragmatism, reality, swallowed
up in forces far more insistent.

He resisted her, rearing up on one elbow, his blue eyes
half-desperate, half-amused. 'Don't, Nicola!'

'But you gave me so much!'

'And found happiness in the giving,' he said, running
his palm over the swell of her hip, then easing his body
away from hers. 'Neither of us is ready for you to get
pregnant. You've got two more years of university and
I've got—well, I've got things to sort out, too.'

How could he sound so practical after such astounding
intimacy? Nicola gazed at him in perplexity, seeing once
again the smooth, broad shoulders, the flat belly corded

with muscles, the long-fingered hands that had sought out all the hidden places of her body. She wanted so badly to say those three little words, I love you, but again something held her back. The knowledge that she did not know what things he had to sort out, and was afraid to ask? The knowledge that in many ways he still was a stranger to her?

Or did it have nothing to do with Trent and everything to do with her own self-doubts?

She did not want to analyse the reasons any more than she wanted to leave Trent's bed. Generosity and courage fusing into a decision, she reached up and kissed him full on the mouth, allowing her kiss to express all the confidence he had given her in her womanhood; for Trent was not holding back because he did not want her. Then, with deliberate sensuality, she wrapped her fingers around his maleness. His instant, involuntary response, transmitted through her fingertips, was both reassurance and a source of pride. The same response flared in his face as she moved her hands gently and insistently, her very lack of skill a provocation in itself.

'Nicola——'

'Please...' she said softly. 'Please, Trent.'

She watched the tension gather in his face, his head thrown back, his body taut. And then, for him, as for her, came that sudden, irreversible plunge into completion. He gripped her shoulders, his breathing harsh against her throat; the pounding of his heart bound him to her. Then he cried out her name, once, twice, and collapsed into her arms. Nicola held him with all her strength and knew she had never been happier in all her life.

The slow minutes passed. Trent's hip was digging into her belly, and to Nicola's inner amusement, for it did not seem to fit the script, she realised she was also ravenously hungry. Wondering if Trent had fallen asleep, she whispered his name.

He raised his head and lifted his weight from her. Not meeting her eyes, playing with her hair where it curled around her ear, he said with an attempt at a laugh which did not quite come off, 'I see now why we hide behind barriers...letting them down can be shattering.'

Nicola took his face in her hands. 'Are you all right?'

'Yeah...I guess so. That's the first time in my life I've opened to a woman. Allowed a woman to reach my soul.'

He was still avoiding her eyes. Nicola remembered the small boy Trent, who had met so much rejection and hatred, and was suddenly afraid. 'You complete me,' she said fiercely. 'As I complete you.'

'Maybe...I'm not sure of anything right now.'

He sounded utterly exhausted and a very long way away. Wanting only to comfort him, yet sure her smile must look artificial, Nicola said, 'Do you know what? I'm starving hungry.'

He not only did not question the smile, he looked relieved by her statement. 'Let's raid the kitchen,' he suggested, rolling off the bed.

Feeling terrifyingly alone, Nicola scrambled off the other side of the bed and began gathering her clothes. Trent's voice was almost natural when, fully dressed, he reached out one hand. 'I know where the cook keeps the raisin bread and the pepperoni.'

She rolled her eyes. 'What a combination!'

'Sex gives you an appetite.'

Nicola did not like him using that small three-letter word to describe what had happened between them in the bed. But all she said was, 'You've got to find some pickled onions if I'm going to eat pepperoni.'

Like two children, they stole into the kitchen at the big house and munched on pepperoni and cheese and raisin bread; and when they got back to the cabin, without a word being spoken, they went to their separate beds.

CHAPTER NINE

THE next morning Nicola woke at dawn. She got out of bed as quietly as she could and slipped into her working clothes. Then she turned on the computer. Flint and Maryanne had yet to make love because her imagination, fertile though it was, had boggled before that final intimacy. Not giving herself time to think, she began to type, letting the words come from somewhere other than her conscious mind as her fingers skipped over the keys.

From a long way away she heard the familiar sounds from next door as Trent got up. Then he climbed her steps. 'Nicola? Coming for breakfast?'

'Later,' she called. 'I'm working right now,' and was not even aware of him descending the stairs.

It was nine-thirty when she finished the scene. Without editing it at all, she pushed the print button and watched the pages scroll off the printer. Then she sat down in the chair to read them.

At first there was a pleased smile on her face, for Flint and Maryanne were indulging in the kind of verbal sparring that was actually giving out a very different message than the words would have implied; she had managed that rather well, she thought, and read on. However, gradually her smile faded, to be replaced by a look of utter consternation. For Flint, dark-haired green-eyed Flint, suddenly had streaked blond hair and eyes the blue of a summer sky.

But worse was to come. Flint's caresses, his softly spoken endearments, were not original to him. They were the caresses Trent had given Nicola in the bed next door, and the words Trent had whispered into her ear. As though she had been in a trance in front of the computer, she had poured out all her wonder and joy in Trent's lovemaking. But more than that, she had also written a very explicit description of it.

With one difference. A very vital difference. For as Maryanne lay, satiated, on Flint's broad chest, she had murmured those three small but so significant words, 'I love you'.

Nicola got to her feet so abruptly that the joined sheets of paper tumbled to the floor. Leaving them there, she started pacing back and forth, back and forth. She had been caught in her own story. Trent had become hero to her heroine, and the words of Maryanne were suddenly her own words. She, Nicola, was in love with Trent. She had been for days, she saw that now, but she'd been too afraid to admit it. It had taken the workings of her subconscious, creative self to tell her the truth.

And Trent loved her; he had said so. Nicola stood still in the middle of the floor, her eyes glowing, her face lit by an involuntary smile. The happy ending, obligatory for her book, would be hers. She loved and was loved.

What more could she ask?

She grinned foolishly at the papers on the floor and suddenly discovered that, once again, she was ravenously hungry. Nothing to do with sex, she thought, and everything to do with love. Playing the words over in her mind—*Trent, I love you . . . I love you, Trent*—she checked her dwindling food supply. The bread had gone mouldy and the cheese was stale. Remembering how hungry she had felt last night in Trent's bed, and how the two of them had giggled like children as they had raided the refrigerator, she decided she would head for the kitchen again. Surely she could talk the cooks into a couple of pieces of toast. And she would probably see

Trent on the way. She could tell him what she had discovered. How wonderful that would be!

Humming to herself, she went outside, leaving the wooden door open, the screen creaking shut. It was another beautiful day. Breathing deeply of the scent of pine and knowing she would always associate it with an intensity and purity of happiness such as she had never known before, Nicola set off through the trees.

Something in the quality of Nicola's smile caused the cook to give her bacon and waffles smothered in maple syrup. Nicola cleaned the plate, drank two cups of coffee and decided to head back to the cabin. She had missed Trent on the way over; she might be luckier on the way back. And, more prosaically, she had a scene to rewrite. There was no way that Flint and Maryanne could so blatantly reveal Nicola's private life, blithely ignoring the boundaries between fact and fiction. Their lovemaking had to come from Nicola's imagination, not from her experience.

She walked back to the cabin more slowly. Trent did not wear tight leather trousers and silk shirts open to the navel as Flint did. Nor was he a rich and powerful business magnate like Flint. Trent's power, she decided thoughtfully, came from within. In jeans, a mud-stained T-shirt and work boots, Trent exuded power. Enough power, magnetism and sexuality for any hero.

She crossed the clearing, walked up her steps, and pulled the door open. Then she stopped dead. Trent was standing in the middle of the living-room, the bundle of paper that was the lovemaking scene in his hand. As she blushed scarlet and made a tiny horror-stricken sound, he looked across the room at her; she had never seen such anger in a man's face.

She said the first thing that came into her head. 'What are you doing here?'

With a wolfish smile Trent indicated a huge sheaf of delphiniums, of azure, purple, and palest blue, lying on the desk. 'I came to bring you these, and then when you weren't home I thought I'd leave them on your desk. To inspire you. But I can see you're in no need of inspiration.'

'Don't be angry!' she gasped. 'I'm going to change——'

'Why change it, Nicola?' he snarled. 'It reads so convincingly. Almost as if you'd been there.'

'I didn't mean to write it that way,' she faltered. 'It just happened.'

'Sure. And your hero just happened to have blond hair and blue eyes. Pure coincidence, of course.'

Incurably honest, she blurted, 'When I started the book, he did. But——'

'Yeah, I bet he did. You've been using me all summer, haven't you? I suppose I should be flattered to figure as the hero in your novel—but oddly enough I'm not.'

'You're not the hero! He's different,' she cried desperately.

He advanced on her, waving the papers in front of her nose. 'If this is anything to go by, he doesn't seem too different to me. There he is in bed, with my moves, my words...and you call that different?'

His face was scored with a contempt so bitter that Nicola was petrified. She managed to gasp, 'Trent, please listen to me. *Please...*'

'I don't even want to be in the same room with you! I thought enough of our relationship to figure you'd at least have the discretion to keep it to yourself. Instead of which you're prepared to expose it in every bookshop across the country—just so you can make a few bucks. And to think I was taken in by you, with your big brown eyes and your air of innocence.' In a gesture that terrified her in its violence, he crumpled the papers into a ball and flung them to the floor. 'It isn't just that I've been deceived—though that would be bad enough. No, I was fool enough to fall in love with you as well...how you must have laughed!'

Wondering if she would ever be able to laugh again, for her body felt as heavy as lead and her throat muscles seemed to be paralysed, Nicola swallowed hard and said in a harsh voice she scarcely recognised as her own, 'You've got it all wrong.'

He ignored her. 'I bet there was one episode you had to leave out,' he sneered. 'What about the thunderstorm, Nicola? I'm quite sure your hero—what was his name, Flint?—isn't afraid of thunderstorms. Did you have to edit that one out? Or did you just twist it round to suit your purposes?'

He was waiting for an answer; and she had no idea what to say. Into the leaden silence, a silence that seemed to last forever, Nicola said in a cracked voice, 'That scene—the one in the bedroom—just wrote itself. This morning. I didn't really have anything to do with it.'

She heard the words replay in her head, and in utter despair wondered if they sounded as unconvincing to Trent as they did to her. 'I know that doesn't make much sense,' she stumbled on, flinching from the burning anger in his eyes. 'But it's the truth! I wouldn't have left that in the book, of course I wouldn't. You've got to believe me!'

'I don't believe you,' he said heavily. 'I don't believe one word. Although I am beginning to understand why you didn't say you loved me. I suppose I should be grateful that you spared me that hypocrisy at least.'

It hardly seemed the time to tell him that she had changed her mind. Wringing her hands, Nicola cried incoherently, 'You aren't Flint! You aren't! In the beginning, yes, when I was angry with you, I did model my hero on you—it was because of the energy that always seemed to be between us. But in the very first chapter Flint became himself, his own person—nothing like you. You must believe that!'

Trent gave an ugly laugh. 'Sure,' he said sarcastically. 'Now let me tell you something, Nicola Shea. You put me in your book and I'll sue you within an inch of your life. I'm damned if I'm having my private life put into print for anyone who's got the price of a paperback. Do you hear me?'

He did not believe one word she had said. Nicola stared at him, her face blank, and deep inside her stirred the bitter knowledge that for the third time she was going to lose the man she loved. Except that her feelings for George and for Allan had been only pale shadows of her feelings for Trent. And this was her own fight, quite unrelated to her sisters.

I've got nothing to lose, she thought. Absolutely nothing. She said evenly, 'Yes, I hear you. But you haven't heard me. I was condemned before I came in the door, wasn't I? Or did you have doubts about me anyway, and this just gave you the opportunity to indulge in them?'

Finally she had his attention. 'What the hell do you mean by that?'

Rashly she pressed on. 'If my mother had died when I was born and I'd been brought up by a grandmother like yours, I'd probably be pretty wary of trusting anyone female. Is that why you've never married, Trent? Never even let a woman close to you? Because you're afraid that we're all wicked grandmothers under the skin?'

His eyes narrowed in fury. Seizing her by the shoulders, he said between gritted teeth, 'Lay off the two-bit psychology.'

'You don't want to hear it because it's the truth!' she retorted. 'And now it's all worked out very nicely, hasn't it? You've been proved right. Nicola's like the rest of them—not to be trusted.' With heavy irony she finished, '*What* a good thing you didn't risk getting me pregnant.'

For several aching seconds Trent said nothing at all. Standing straight under the weight of his hands, Nicola decided with one small part of her brain that he looked murderous. No other word for it. Refusing to quail, she glared back at him. With a muttered exclamation he flung himself away from her. 'I don't have to listen to this! Just remember what I said—put any of this stuff into print, and I'll sue.'

You don't have a worry in the world, she thought with desperate humour. Because Flint with his silk shirts is no one you'd recognise. He's nothing like you at all.

She was standing in the middle of the room; Trent was between her and the door, a beam of sunlight catching in his hair and deepening the blue of his eyes. He said with an ugly ring in his voice, 'Maybe I shouldn't be in too much of a hurry to leave. We could make love again—after all, it might broaden your range of adjectives and adverbs. Add a few more paragraphs to what you've already written. How about it?'

Deep within her she felt a quiver of terror. 'No!' she said. 'I'd hate that.'

'Come on, Nicola, you've got to be willing to sacrifice for the cause of art.' He stepped towards her, out of the beam of light.

She said tightly, 'You come one step nearer and I'll scream my head off, Trent. I mean it.'

'How melodramatic,' he said smoothly. 'I hope, by the way, you've been taking mental notes of this conversation—could be useful, couldn't it?'

'It's a scene that's gone on much too long,' she retorted, visited with the certain knowledge that she was going to cry if he didn't go soon.

'I've already suggested it needs a little action rather than all this dialogue.'

'The only appropriate action is for you to leave.'

'So you can get to work?' His eyes impaled her, as unyielding as steel. 'If I just walk tamely out of the door, that's rather a flat ending to this particular scene, wouldn't you agree? I think it needs a little pepping up.'

Before she could guess his intentions, he had pulled her roughly into his arms and was kissing her, a raw, angry kiss fuelled by an inward ferocity, a kiss which seemed to go on forever; and the worst thing about it was that at some deep level all the passion he had awoken in her yesterday leaped instantly into life. Then he thrust her away. 'That should make a better ending,' he grated, and lunged out of the door.

Nicola stood still; she was not sure she could have moved had she wanted to. There were no further sounds from next door, so Trent must have headed for the house. She was alone.

She could make a happy ending for Flint and Maryanne. But for herself and Trent there was not to be one. Instead there was the harsh agony of an ending too close to the beginning, of an ending that should never have been.

A week passed, during which Nicola lost three pounds and all the colour in her cheeks. She developed violet-blue shadows under her eyes, jumped if anyone laid a finger on her, and worked like a woman possessed. The same day that she had written the love scene between Flint and Maryanne she had erased it from her screen, unable to as much as look at it again. The rewrite was adequate although not inspired; she got rid of some of her pent-up emotion when Maryanne had an unexpected and thoroughly convincing fight with Flint.

Two days after her own fight with Trent, she had gone to see Olivia. Olivia was seated behind her desk, wearing a severe black jumpsuit and quantities of turquoise jewellery, her eyeshadow exactly matching the polished stones. Nicola closed the door firmly and said without finesse, 'Olivia, I want to move out of the cabin into the room in the attic.'

Olivia tilted her head to one side. 'You can't,' she said. 'I'm using it for storage space.'

Nicola had not expected a refusal. 'I'll move the stuff out myself. Please, Olivia?'

'It's much too heavy to be moved again—I had to get Trent and Daniel to put it there in the first place. What's wrong with the cabin all of a sudden, Nicola? I thought you were happy there.'

This was a question Nicola had expected. 'Trent and I aren't getting along very well,' she said with apparent frankness. 'I thought it would be easier for both of us if we didn't live so close together.' This explanation was euphemistic, to put it mildly. It had been torture the last forty-eight hours hearing Trent move around next door, listening to the rhythm of his breathing at night while she lay wide awake in the darkness, knowing all his comings and goings yet never once exchanging a word with him.

'Had a fight, did you?' Olivia said callously. 'Well, you're young—you'll either make up or get over it.'

Nicola had had four hours' sleep the night before and had been snubbed by Trent at the breakfast table. 'You're a horrible old woman,' she choked.

'Trent needs you,' Olivia said obliquely.

'Trent needs me like he needs a hole in the head!' Nicola gave Olivia a scorching look and heard the words trip from her tongue. 'Did you happen to know his grandmother?'

'My sister. Died ten years ago. Not much loss.'

Somehow not surprised by this information, Nicola asked with an urgency that took her by surprise, 'What was she like?'

'Evil,' said Olivia, giving the archaic word its due weight. 'She hated Trent from the moment he was born. It's a tribute to his strength that he survived her.'

Nicola leaned over the desk, her eyes blazing. 'And where were you when she was locking him in the root cellar?'

'So you know about that, do you? Well, well...' Olivia rubbed the polished surface of the turquoise on her finger. 'The gardener told me what was going on—unfortunately not until it had happened several times. So I told my sister I'd set the authorities on her, make the biggest scandal in the county, if she didn't send Trent to a boarding-school. And I made sure it was a very good boarding-school.'

Nicola slowly expelled her breath. 'I see...I didn't know that.'

'Not much of a talker, Trent.'

'I didn't even know how he earned his living until he told me one day he's an architect.'

'And a very good one. He built the standard sort of stuff at first and made a lot of money in the Calgary oil boom days. Now he's into quality—but not for the rich. Quality with the lowest possible price tag. Nursing homes built on one floor so that all the rooms look out over shrubs and flowers. Apartment buildings cantilevered so all the occupants can have a roof garden and a view— harmony with the environment, in other words, at a price

ordinary people can afford . . . he's extremely good at his
job, and highly respected.'

Storing all this information away, Nicola said, 'So why
is he mowing your lawns, Olivia?'

'You'd better ask him, hadn't you?' Olivia burnished
the turquoise on her sleeve. 'Off you go now, Nicola,
I've got things to do.'

Nicola knew Olivia well enough not to waste time
arguing. Her picture of Trent had filled out considerably; and Olivia had said Trent needed her.

But, she thought, walking down the path between the
purple trumpets of the petunias, if he doesn't think so,
it doesn't do me much good. Nor, as the slow summer
days passed, did Trent give any indication of need. He
continued to ignore her as thoroughly as if she did not
exist, as if she were totally transparent and he could see
right through her.

Then, on a Wednesday evening an hour after dinner,
someone tapped on her door. Nicola was sitting at the
computer. When she looked up and saw it was Trent
standing outside, her fingers glued themselves to the keys,
giving her a line of gibberish, and her heart performed
a most uncomfortable somersault in her chest. Before
she could say anything he said coldly, 'Phone call for
you up at the house. It's long distance, you'd better
hurry.'

'Oh . . . thanks,' she stammered. But she said it to an
empty space. Trent had already gone. Torn between
wanting to cry her eyes out or scream imprecations after
him, she pushed the save button and turned off the
computer.

She had no idea who would be phoning her. Thrusting
her feet into deck shoes, she hurried through the trees
to the main house and climbed the stairs to the cubicle.

The telephone receiver was dangling from the hook. Nicola picked it up and said, 'Hello?'

'Nikki? It's Cheryl. Can Gayle and I come and visit you this weekend?'

Nicola had not spoken to Cheryl for at least three months; but Cheryl disliked the phone, perhaps sensing that her beauty was wasted on a telephone line, and consequently always came right to the point. 'Sure,' said Nicola, 'I'd love to see you both.' Her sisters, for all their faults, had always been good company, and two familiar faces from home would cheer her up. Trent was lost to her anyway, so what did it matter?

'We've got a week's vacation. We could fly into Deer Lake on Friday, stay for a couple of days, and then fly to St John's. Could you meet us at the airport?'

Nicola thought fast. 'I don't have a car. But Olivia would probably lend me the truck.'

'A truck?' Cheryl repeated. Cheryl liked sports cars.

'A truck,' Nicola replied firmly. 'This isn't a luxury resort. And I might have to work some of the time you're here.'

'That's all right,' Cheryl said airily. 'We'll find something to amuse ourselves.'

Nicola had no doubt of it; and no doubt that the something would be male. Trying to ignore a sinking feeling in the vicinity of her stomach, she got details of flight times and said she would call right back if a vehicle was not available. Then she went to see Olivia. Olivia had raved over chapters eight and nine; Olivia surely would have no objection to lending her the truck.

'When?' said Olivia. 'Friday? That's no problem, there are some boxes of mine due in on a flight from Toronto tomorrow. Instead of getting them then, Trent can pick them up on Friday—and you can go with him to get your sisters.'

Her smile was as smooth as cream. Nicola said calmly, 'I have a better idea. I'll pick up the boxes...that way I won't be tearing Trent away from the garden.'

Olivia gave her undignified cackle and the emerald on her finger winked. 'Nice try,' she said. 'But these are very heavy packages, too heavy for you to manage on your own. You can have the truck with Trent, or neither one.'

'If you're trying to matchmake, Olivia, it's a lost cause!'

Olivia looked pointedly at the papers on her desk. 'You'll look after the arrangements with Trent, won't you?' she said, and picked up her pen.

Nicola marched out of the office and headed straight for the tool shed, where she had seen Trent bent over the lawnmower on her way over; if she waited to speak to him, she would lose her nerve. She walked right up to him and said in an expressionless voice, 'My sisters are flying into Deer Lake on Friday—Olivia says I can go with you to the airport. The plane gets in at three.'

She was scowling at him. He said coldly, 'I would gather this was not your idea.'

'It was not.'

'The truck's got a double cab, so it'll seat four. We'll leave around one-thirty.' Turning away from her, he punctured a hole in a small can of oil and added it to the red plastic gas container.

Nicola left.

CHAPTER TEN

FRIDAY arrived all too soon. Nicola forced herself to concentrate on chapter eleven all morning, rushed through her lunch, then hurried back to the cabin, where she showered, brushed her hair into short wispy curls, and dressed in a full green skirt with a white blouse embroidered with big green and pink flowers. She added her green sandals, Mexican silver earrings and a generous coating of pink lipstick. She was ready.

War paint, she thought ruefully, and wondered if it was for Trent's benefit or her sisters'. Looping a fleecy green sweater round her shoulders, for the sky was overcast and the breeze had a sea chill to it, she headed for the house. Trent was sitting in the truck waiting for her. She opened the door and climbed in. 'I hope you haven't been waiting long,' she said politely.

He put the truck in gear, spinning the tyres in the gravel as he accelerated out of the driveway. His profile was closed against her and his chin set. It was obvious he had no intention of replying.

Nicola did up her seatbelt and folded her hands neatly in her lap. 'It's a cool day, isn't it?'

Trent grunted.

Nicola examined her fingernails.

Ten minutes later the truck turned on to the main road, Nicola, who had been thinking furiously, said in a non-committal voice, 'You're sulking.'

Trent shot her a fulminating look. 'It drives me crazy to be this close to you and not know where the hell I stand.'

She said casually, 'I love you, you know.'

His long fingers tightened on the steering wheel. 'Don't play games, Nicola.'

'I'm not. It's the truth. The scene I wrote that you were so angry about—which has long since been consigned to the rubbish bin, you will be glad to know—that scene was how I discovered I loved you.'

'I don't want to talk about it.'

She took a deep breath. 'Trent, as a small boy you were driven inside yourself in order to survive. But now it's time to come out. You love me, you say——'

'Loved.'

Her nails dug into her palm. 'You're not that changeable,' she said, praying that her words were true. 'But loving me means trusting me as well. You can't have one without the other. That scene you read *was* about you and me. I knew it as soon as I read it, and so did you. But I swear I didn't write it that way...it wrote itself, and in so doing showed me how I feel about you.'

'Considering you've had several days, and that you write fiction, I would have thought you could have come up with a more convincing explanation than that.'

Nicola bit her lip. Courage, she thought. Hold on to your courage. 'Trent, you showed me so much love when we made love...so much tenderness. Don't lock that all away again. Please don't!'

'You really are afraid I'll sue, aren't you?'

Nicola's breath hissed between her teeth. In the eight months with Gran she had learned patience. But there were limits. 'You're being hateful! Absolutely hateful.'

'So stop talking to me.'

'I don't even want to be in the truck with you! Live in your tight little world, Trent. Believe all women are like your grandmother—and see if I care.' After which childish—and quite untrue—outburst, Nicola edged as far away from him as she could in the confines of the seatbelt and stared out at the passing trees. Her sisters were welcome to him, she thought bitterly. They could have him and good luck to them.

However, when she and Trent got to the small cluster of buildings near the runway and went into the terminal, the television monitor announced that the flight was ten minutes late. Trent said coolly, 'That'll give me time to get Olivia's parcels from the freight department,' turned away from her and nearly bumped into a short, heavy-set man who had been advancing on him with hand outstretched.

The man said jovially, 'Trent! Wonderful to see you. But what brings you to this neck of the woods—this is your busiest time of the year, isn't it?'

Nicola turned around as well. The man was wearing an expensively tailored summerweight suit that could not quite disguise the outward signs of too much good eating, while his haircut, his shoes, the gold watch on his wrist— another Piaget, she thought with wicked accuracy—all spoke money. His surprise at seeing Trent was genuine enough; the false note was the smile. As he stood confidently waiting for an explanation, she sensed undercurrents whose source she had no idea of.

Trent said smoothly, 'Mortimer! Good to see you . . . I could ask the same question of you, you know.' And he laughed.

It was a frank, casual laugh that to Nicola's ears also rang false. Mortimer said succinctly, 'Offshore oil. Big opportunities. But you're not interested in oil, Trent.'

Trent put an arm around Nicola's shoulders, drawing her close to his side, and said, 'Vacation, Mortimer— we're leaving later today. I'd like you to meet Nicola Flint. Mortimer Tate, Nicola.'

Not even blinking at her sudden change of name, Nicola held out her hand. Mortimer shook it with a flourish and said gallantly, 'You always did have excellent taste, Trent.'

Feeling a bit as though she had been compared to a piece of furniture, or else a clutch of other women, Nicola said composedly, 'You've known Trent for some time then, Mr Tate?'

'We go back a long way, yes.' For a moment quite another emotion showed in Mortimer Tate's small dark eyes. Then he focused on Nicola again. 'You're from Calgary, Miss Flint?'

Before she could answer, Trent said lightly, 'We're going to have to leave you, Mortimer—we've got to make arrangements to ship some lobster. Nice seeing you, and good luck with the oil.'

He dropped his arm from Nicola's shoulders and took her by the elbow, pushing her purposefully towards the exit. 'Goodbye, Mr Tate,' she called over her shoulder. 'Safe journey.' Then, as the glass doors closed behind them, she hissed, 'You tell lies with altogether too much facility, Trent Livingstone. Would you kindly explain what that was all about?'

'He's the last person I would have chosen to meet right now,' Trent said grimly. 'And no, I can't.'

He was striding towards the freight shed. Hurrying to keep up with him, Nicola said, 'I don't see why a man like Mortimer Tate should be any threat to a highly successful Calgary architect who has police connections.'

Trent stopped so suddenly that she cannoned into him. His eyes like ice, he grated, 'What do you know about the police?'

The man standing in front of her was the same man who had so frightened her in the shower; but Nicola had travelled a long way since that day. 'I overheard you on the telephone...I was in the library.'

'You're too curious for your own good!'

Limpidly she widened her eyes. 'You never did look at home pushing a lawnmower. Since you didn't embezzle your grandmother's fortune, I'm left to wonder what you have done that necessitates hiding behind Olivia's admittedly very decorative skirts.'

Trent said a short, pithy word that made Nicola blink. Then he added, 'All you're getting is my standard reply—mind your own business.'

'But Trent, you've just ruined my reputation as far as Mortimer's concerned. I'm a fallen woman. Vacationing with a man to whom I am not legally married. Travelling under a false name.' Thoroughly enjoying herself, Nicola put the back of her hand to her forehead and reeled in fake horror.

'You're attracting attention,' Trent said drily.

'I attract attention whenever I'm with you because you're so handsome and sexy.'

The grimness left his mouth, replaced by a reluctant smile. 'You know damn well you attract attention because you're a very beautiful woman.'

'So together we're quite a combination,' she said agreeably.

His smile faded. 'Look, this is all very amusing, Nicola—but that man could be dangerous. I mean that. If he's still in the terminal when you go back, please don't tell him your real name or where we're staying.'

Nicola knew well enough when not to ask questions. 'I won't,' she said.

'Thanks.'

Trent smiled again, a real smile that warmed his eyes and softened the harsh lines of his face. Without warning Nicola felt a pang of desire so strong that instinctively she swayed towards him; and saw reflected in his face the same fierce need.

The wind chased a tattered sheet of newsprint across the tarmac, and with a scream of flaps a plane landed on the runway. Trent said bluntly, 'Do you lie awake on your side of the wall as I do on mine?'

'Yes,' she said.

'The issue isn't if I trust you,' he went on, so quietly she had to strain for the words. 'It's if I can trust myself enough to trust you.'

His shoulders were hunched and his fists thrust in his pockets in a pose she recognised. She could feel his conflict as if it were her own, and knew it was his to resolve; she could not do it for him. Wishing his grandmother could appear in front of her for just five minutes, she said in as normal a voice as she could manage, 'Why don't you get the parcels and I'll check to see if Mortimer has gone through security?'

He nodded and turned on his heel, and Nicola walked back to the terminal. When she looked through the glass door she saw Mortimer talking animatedly into one of the telephones on the far wall, and with a sense of premonition knew it was something to do with Trent. She stepped back out of sight, waited two or three minutes and looked again. The telephone booth was empty and the back of a smart summerweight suit was just vanishing through security. She pushed open the door and walked in.

Her sisters' flight had arrived; it must have been the plane that had landed while she was outside. She stood to one side to wait while the passengers began to trickle through the door, gradually filling the room, clustering round the baggage carousels. Children, released from cramped seats, were running around screaming; couples embraced. Gayle and Cheryl were among the last to arrive. For a moment Nicola watched them, feeling a strong surge of affection.

Gayle was wearing a very short, very smart linen suit with gleaming Italian court shoes, her sleek chestnut hair also gleaming; her legs were beautiful. Cheryl, whose legs were not as beautiful but whose breasts had caused more than one man to lose his self-control, was still in her waif phase; her loose flowered sundress was almost floor-length, although it revealed a generous amount of cleavage and bared the shoulders where her red curls tumbled artlessly. Had the airlines allowed it, she would have been bare-foot. While Gayle made men think of satin sheets and champagne, Cheryl brought to mind tumbles in the hay on sun-drenched summer afternoons.

Nicola pushed her way through the crowd and threw her arms around them. 'Wonderful to see you both!' she cried.

Gayle, who did not want her suit mussed, held her at arm's length and said thoughtfully, 'You look different. More sure of yourself.'

'Prettier,' said Cheryl and hugged Nicola again.

As they waited for the baggage, the three of them chattered about the flight, Mexican jewellery, and the nightclubs in Halifax, which were apparently proving most satisfactory. Then Cheryl said, 'Are we really driving in a truck?'

'With a chauffeur,' Nicola said, and tilted her chin. 'He's mine—although he's fighting it. So hands off, you two.'

'Where is he?' Cheryl demanded.

'What does he look like?' Gayle added, automatically smoothing her hair.

Nicola searched through the crowd for Trent's tall figure. 'Maybe he's still out in the freight shed,' she said uncertainly.

Then she saw him push open the glass door and stand for a moment, looking at her. A small boy of perhaps three or four was running towards him, waving a red truck over his head and screeching excitedly; the child ran straight into Trent's legs, catapulted backwards, sat down hard on the floor and began to cry.

As Trent automatically knelt to pick him up, Nicola said, 'That's him. By the door.'

'Wow,' said Cheryl.

'Well,' said Gayle. 'Introduce us.'

'Right now,' said Cheryl.

'Mine,' repeated Nicola, and led the way through the crowd.

As they got a little closer Nicola could hear the boy wailing for his truck, which had also crashed to the floor. Trent reached over for it, and a wheel fell off. The child cried harder. Awkwardly Trent put an arm around the little boy. 'Are you hurt?'

'Truck's broke,' sobbed the boy.

'Don't cry—I can fix it,' Trent said reassuringly.

The tears dried. 'Fix it,' the child ordered, his lip quivering.

Trent fiddled with the axle, pushed on the wheel and then handed the truck back. The child gave the truck a good shake, directed an angelic smile full at Trent, and ran away, waving the truck as if it were an aeroplane. Trent slowly straightened, watching him go, his face twisted with an emotion as strong as it was unnameable.

But Nicola knew what it signified: Trent was remembering another small boy, one whom no one had picked up or hugged or comforted. She cleared her throat loudly and called, 'Trent! We're over here.'

The emotion was wiped from his face as if a cloth had passed over it. His eyes moved from Nicola to Gayle's slim elegance and on to Cheryl's enticing disorder.

'You're Nicola's sisters,' he said and held out his hand. 'Trent Livingstone.'

Gayle, the eldest, took it first in her cool fingers with their cluster of expensive rings. 'I'm delighted to meet you,' she said, and her grey-green eyes calmly ran over his features and came to rest on the strongly sculpted mouth. Lightly her fingers increased their pressure.

Cheryl, not used to being ignored and never as subtle as Gayle, let her bag slip off her shoulder and drop to the floor. She and Trent reached for it at the same time, and she thereby presented him with a deliberate view of her breasts. Her bare arm brushed his. 'I'm Cheryl . . . thanks so much, I didn't mean to drop it,' she said with a breathy laugh and a look in her eyes that said, Where have you been all my life?

Trent moved his arm away from hers, smiled at Nicola and said, 'Perhaps we should get the luggage.'

Only slightly comforted by the smile, Nicola trailed behind. Her stomach was in knots, and she had the horrible sense of history repeating itself: George in his white medical coat and bearded Allan with his philosophy texts were very clear in her mind. Gayle was walking on Trent's right side and Cheryl on his left; both of them looked absolutely stunning, she thought, and felt a return of the old sense of helplessness that had dogged her teenage years.

For a moment it almost won. Then her spine stiffened. She was not sixteen or nineteen or even twenty-one. She was twenty-three, nor was she prepared to allow either or both of her sisters to commandeer Trent from under her nose.

The suitcases were sliding down the ramp on to the carousel. Nicola slipped her arm through Trent's, felt the muscles tense, and prayed he would not push her away.

Gayle said calmly, 'There's mine,' indicating an Italian leather bag. 'And mine,' added Cheryl of a bulging canvas haversack.

Trent dropped Nicola's arm and picked up the bags. The three of them edged their way out of the terminal and walked to the car park, Cheryl chattering insouciantly, Gayle interposing the occasional dry comment. Nicola watched the play of muscles in Trent's bare forearms and wondered why love should cause so much misery.

Trent heaved the bags into the back of the truck. 'It's going to be a bit cramped in the cab,' he said.

'I'll sit in the front with you,' said Gayle, with the candid, direct look that hinted of more favours to come and that rarely failed her.

Cheryl ran her fingers through her curls and said with a charming pout, 'I think Trent should decide who sits in the front.'

And Nicola, in a flash, saw that she could not hold Trent if he did not want to be held. She waited, her heart beating very fast, to see what he would decide.

Trent leaned against the side of the truck, his long body perfectly relaxed, looked from Gayle to Cheryl and said, 'Let's get something straight—it'll save time and energy if we do. You're two very beautiful women; I'm by no means blind to that. But I'm not interested.'

Cheryl said regretfully, 'Not the tiniest bit?'

'Not at all,' said Trent.

'Why not?' Gayle asked, giving him a cool, assessing look.

'I happen to find your sister more beautiful then either of you.'

'Are you going to marry her?' Cheryl demanded. But Trent hesitated for too long in replying, and she pounced on him with all the ferocity of a wolf protecting her cub. 'Why aren't you?'

'He doesn't trust me,' Nicola interposed, rather tired of being left out of the conversation.

Cheryl threw back her head and hooted, and Gayle allowed herself an amused smile before saying, 'If you don't trust Nicola, Mr Livingstone, you don't trust anyone.'

Cheryl said, 'She never ever cheated in school.'

Gayle added, 'She couldn't tell lies. She'd get red in the face instead.'

'She was the one who stayed home and looked after our grandmother when she was ill.'

'She's always been wonderful with children, and children know who can be trusted.'

'*We* think you should marry her,' Cheryl finished, tossing her hair.

'It would certainly seem you're the right man for her,' Gayle corroborated.

'And why do you say that?' Trent asked, with what Nicola called his inscrutable look.

'You're the first one of her serious boyfriends we haven't been able to—er—distract,' Gayle said, her carmined lips still with that faint smile.

Nicola, who had been sputtering incoherently in the background, said loudly, 'Do you mean to say that you two took George and Allan away on *purpose*?'

'We had to look after you,' Cheryl put in. 'You weren't like us—we were born knowing the score.'

Gayle shrugged her linen-clad shoulders. 'Anyway, if they'd been the right men, they wouldn't have gone with us, would they?'

'You might have told me!'

Cheryl frowned in unaccustomed thought. 'Wasn't it obvious?'

'No! I just thought I was a failure as a woman.'

Gayle looked at Cheryl, who looked back. 'Oh, dear,' said Gayle.

'We're sorry,' Cheryl cried, hugging her sister.

'But it's all worked out for the best,' Gayle said. 'Because Trent is different.' She smiled at him, a lazy, heavy-lidded smile. 'And well worth waiting for, I would say.' Then, with an abrupt switch to a businesslike air, she added, 'Come on, Cheryl, we'll get in the back.'

Trent opened the door for them and said casually, 'You won't be bored at the Eyrie, I'll guarantee that. Daniel, I'm sure, will be susceptible... and then there's always Rafe and Tad.'

Nicola smothered a laugh at the thought of Gayle, Cheryl and Suzie all circling the unsuspecting Daniel, and climbed in the front of the truck.

Gayle's and Cheryl's visit passed all too quickly. Trent moved to a folding bed in the kitchen, keeping his distance for the whole weekend. Nicola tried very hard to label this as tact and revealed as little as she could to her highly inquisitive sisters about the uneven path of her relationship with him. This was not easy, but she managed. In the meantime the three of them took over the whole cabin, giggling and telling stories until two in the morning and eating far too many of Cheryl's homemade chocolate chip cookies.

Olivia raised no demur when Nicola asked for the truck to drive back to Deer Lake on Sunday evening. At the airport the three sisters exchanged affectionate hugs and promises to get together more often. Then Nicola drove home through the dusk. Trent would have moved back to his side of the cabin by now... would she see him that night? Or was he still afraid to trust himself to the intimacy and energy and wonder that, for want of a better word, was called love?

The wind was high that evening, and by the time Nicola had parked the truck and was walking through the pine grove it was dark. The woods were full of mysterious creaks and rustles; boughs brushed her face and whipped at her skirt with pliant fingers. But her eyes grew accustomed to the darkness, and there was a new lift to her step, for the weekend with Gayle and Cheryl had given her back parts of herself she had lost years ago. What a strange summer it had been, she mused, stepping over a twisted root. She had lost her fear of the water. She had made peace with her sisters. She had fallen in love. And all she had come here to do was to write a book so she could make some money.

But then the book itself had been about love...

Ahead of her came the loud snap of a twig, and a smothered curse. Nicola stopped in her tracks, her pulse racing. The voice had not been Trent's.

The wind sighed in the trees. The boughs waved like fans in front of her eyes. Over her head the clouds scudded past a thin crescent moon. No further noises. No sign of human presence. But she had not imagined the voice, she knew she had not. And knew also, with a primitive *frisson* along her spine, that the intruder meant no good.

Very quietly, her eyes seeking out every footstep, Nicola crept forward, and not once did it occur to her that it might have been safer to go back to the house and fetch help. Finding time to be thankful that she had pulled her dark green sweater over her white blouse, she ducked under the low-hanging branches of a maple and saw the lights of the cabin glowing through the trees. So Trent was home.

Her nerves screaming with tension, her eyes flitting from tree to tree in search of she knew not what, Nicola edged along the path, eventually finding a hiding place behind a big, rough-barked pine. She peered around its trunk. She was nearly at the clearing in front of the cabin, so near that the lights were spoiling her night vision.

And then she saw him. A dark bulky shape, crouched in the path, limned by the light from Trent's windows. Visible to her. But invisible to anyone coming out of the cabin.

With a sick plunging of her stomach, she saw something else. The man had a gun. Its long, lethal shape was resting across his arm.

He was waiting for Trent.

In a split second Nicola remembered the furrowed scar on Trent's arm, the strange undercurrents between him and Mortimer Tate, and Mortimer's phone call; and never doubted that these facts were connected.

Very carefully she stooped, and found what she was looking for: a stout fallen limb lying in the undergrowth. But she could not move it without making a noise. She bit her lip, wondering what to do.

Then the problem was solved for her. The screen door opened and Trent stepped outside. Nicola grabbed the branch, screeched a warning at the top of her lungs and launched herself at the man in the path. He twisted round when she yelled; the gun was pointing at the moon. Nicola swung the branch at him, heard an oath that her grandmother would have deplored, and, as he started to his feet, threw herself into his lap.

With a streak of flame and a deafening blast the gun went off. Terrified, Nicola clung to the man as if he were a lover, wrapping her arms around him and holding on with all her strength as he kicked out at her ankles. She saw his raised fist a moment before it struck her, and managed to dodge the worst of the blow; her head ringing, she felt him tear free of her and frantically grabbed for him, sobbing out Trent's name.

'Let go, Nicola—get out of the way!'

It was Trent's voice. Even with the darkness whirling around her, Nicola realised that he sounded both furious and exhilarated. She heard a rather horrible crunch, and then saw Trent stand up, the rifle under his arm.

He was safe. He had not been shot.

With a tiny sigh Nicola closed her eyes. But the whirling was now behind her lids, and she was shivering and trembling like a sick puppy.

'Nicola, are you hurt?'

Warm arms were around her, lifting her up. The hard thudding under her cheek was Trent's heart. 'I'm fine,' she whispered.

'Are you sure? I saw him hit you——'

She spoke the simple truth. 'As long as you're all right, I am, too.'

For a moment Trent stood still at the edge of the trees. 'You really mean that, don't you?' he said in a strange voice. 'God, Nicola, I must have done something right in my life to have found you.'

She nuzzled her face into his chest. 'You give the nicest compliments,' she mumbled. 'They're just kind of rare.'

'Give me time—I've got lots to learn. Although admittedly you shouldn't have to get hit on the head before I give you one.' His arms tightened convulsively. 'Listen—I'm going to take you to the cabin and come back and tie this fellow up . . . chance to practice my boy scout knots. Then you and I have to talk.'

'Yessir,' she murmured.

He was climbing the steps to his side of the cabin; he was also holding the gun, which banged lightly against her leg. 'You're as brave as a lion,' he said. 'You know that?'

'He was going to shoot you. I'm not brave.'

This time Trent managed the doors himself. Keeping a firm hold on her, he walked through the living-room to the bedroom, where he put her down on the bed. 'Stay here,' he ordered. 'I'll be back in a couple of minutes.'

Nicola had never expected to find herself in his bedroom again. 'I'm staying because I want to,' she announced, her eyes huge in a dead-white face. 'Not because you're telling me to.'

'A much preferable state of affairs.'

He was still visibly blazing with energy. Nicola said accusingly, 'You enjoyed hitting that man.'

'He'd just hit you,' Trent said, plainly considering that reason enough. Then he gave himself a little shake and ran his fingers through his hair. 'Besides, it was because of him that I've spent over two months learning a whole lot about gardening that I never really wanted to know— I owed him one. I'll be back in a couple of minutes.'

When he had gone, Nicola swung her legs over the side of the bed and stood up. Rather to her surprise her knees appeared to be functioning. She walked slowly to the bathroom and looked in the mirror. In that brief scuffle on the ground she had got amazingly dirty. Bits of needles and twigs were caught in her hair; her hands, where she had grasped the bough, were grimy; a long streak of dirt marred her cheek and a tender spot on her jaw was already turning an interesting shade of mauve. She turned on the tap and reached for the soap.

She was rinsing her face in cold water when Trent said from the doorway, 'Here, let me do that.'

As she turned her head, the light fell on the bruise on her jaw. He took a cloth, ran it under the cold tap and pressed it gently to the swelling, an expression on his face that she had never seen before and that made her want to cry. He said in a conversational tone of voice, 'I've never done this before, you know—looked after someone. Never wanted to.'

'No one ever looked after you,' Nicola said quietly.

'You would, though, wouldn't you? You'd throw yourself at a man with a loaded gun if he was threatening me, you'd take care of me if I was ill and you'd cheer me on when things were going well. Wouldn't you, Nicola?'

The intensity in his eyes made her tremble. She said in a low voice, 'If you'd let me, Trent.'

'I'd more than let you. I want you to.' He ran the cloth under the cold water again, wringing it out. Then his eyes met hers on the other side of the sink. 'I want you to marry me.'

Nicola gripped the basin, wondering if she was dreaming; the coldness of the porcelain told her she was not. She said steadily, 'Do you love me?'

He dropped the cloth in the sink. 'I don't blame you for asking that. I was lying when I implied I didn't love you any more. Lying to protect myself, lying out of fear. Of course I love you. Maybe I have since the first moment I saw you staring down at me and my whisky bottle with equal disapproval. Maybe that was why I was so desperate to get rid of you, because I was afraid. Nicola, I won't always be easy to live with. I'm new at loving someone, I'll make mistakes and I might hurt you...but I swear you're my heart's desire—you're what I've been looking for all my life and didn't even know it. I'll love you as long as there's breath in my body, I'll worship you with my body, and bringing you joy will make me happier than I ever thought I could be.'

Shaken to her soul, Nicola gazed at him in silence and felt tears well into her eyes. She said huskily, 'Those are the most beautiful things anyone has ever said to me. Olivia should have you writing poetry, not weeding flowerbeds.'

His crooked smile, so familiar to her, lit up his face. 'The poetry is for you, sweetheart, not for Olivia. As is the proposal of marriage. To which you have not replied.'

Her brown eyes clear, she said formally, 'I would like to marry you, Trent. Thank you for asking.'

A grin split his face. 'You don't have a clue why I'm here at the Eyrie, I could be a gangster on the run for all you know, yet you're willing to take that on trust... and to think I didn't trust you!'

'Why are you here?' she said equably.

'You know I'm an architect... recently I did some work for an associate of Mortimer's, a man called Peter Tallon—the man out there in the path whom you were so enthusiastically embracing a few minutes ago. The job was in connection with a shopping mall, and by sheer chance I found out that Peter was using substandard concrete. When I went to him, figuring his contractors had been cheating him, it soon became clear he was the one doing the cheating. I made the mistake of giving him a week to clean up his act before I'd go to the police. Three days later I was nearly run over by a car, and the day after I was shot at when I was out jogging—you were right about the scar, it was a bullet wound. So I went to the police, but I was too late—Peter had skipped town. When there was a fire in my house the following week, the police chief suggested I lie low until they could arrest him, and Olivia offered me a place here... I've always had a soft spot for Olivia.'

'If all that hadn't happened, we would never have met,' Nicola said, awed.

Trent leaned over the basin and kissed the tip of her nose. 'We were destined to meet, my love.'

'Mortimer's the one who leaked where you were,' Nicola said. 'He was on the phone as soon as you left the terminal that day.'

'One of Mortimer's many interests is a cement company—he and Peter have been buddies for years.'

'What an exciting life you architects lead,' said Nicola.

'More exciting than planting petunias.'

Nicola grinned. 'So if we get married you'll do the repairs around the house and I'll raise the delphiniums.'

'What do you mean, if?'

She said honestly, 'I still can't quite believe that all this is happening.'

Trent came round the basin, clasped her in his arms and kissed her so comprehensively that she was left breathless and dishevelled. 'Now do you?' he asked. 'Mind you, if you still have any lingering doubts, we could go back to the bedroom and I could do my best to dispel them.'

Pink-cheeked, Nicola said, 'No doubts whatsoever. But we could go to the bedroom anyway.'

'You're not only beautiful and brave as a lion, you're smart,' he said. 'If you like, I could propose again in the bedroom—the bathroom doesn't seem like the most romantic of settings.'

'Wherever you are is romantic,' she simpered, fluttering her lashes.

'A line straight out of your book.' Trent added ruefully. 'Olivia tore a strip off me the other day about your book. She said in effect that I was not Flint and that you had stringently observed the boundaries between fact and fiction.'

'I've tried to.' She hesitated. 'But in a way you are in my book. My first hero was as dull as ditchwater, and after I met you I knew he wouldn't do. So Flint came into being—he isn't you, yet because you deepened my emotional range and taught me about the power and intensity of love you're partly responsible for him.'

Trent grimaced. 'I'm sorry I was so angry with you about that scene. I couldn't bear the thought that something so shatteringly beautiful to me had only been research to you. So I lost my cool.'

'You're forgiven.' All her feeling for him lighting up her face, Nicola added spontaneously, 'Oh, Trent, I do love you!'

A matching emotion flared in his eyes. 'About time you told me,' he said.

'I've been afraid to. Afraid I'd lose you to my sisters, that I wouldn't be enough for you.'

He laughed. 'You're more than enough, my darling Nicola. Especially when your temper's high.'

'Do you think we'll still fight sometimes?' she asked, head to one side.

'I would suspect we might.'

'I wouldn't want our married life to be dull—although how could it be when I love you so much?' Nicola put her arms around him and hugged him hard. 'You know, there's one more thing we have in common with my book. A happy ending.'

'A happy ending which is only a beginning,' Trent said, kissing her lips with lingering promise. 'If you want to come with me, I'll show you what I mean.'

'All right,' said Nicola. 'I'll do that.'

So it was not until one in the morning that Trent reported an armed assault to the local police, and it was three days before Nicola could settle down to chapter twelve.

Mills & Boon

Next month's Romances

Each month, you can choose from a world of variety in romance with Mills & Boon. These are the new titles to look out for next month.

SOME KIND OF MADNESS Robyn Donald

A FORBIDDEN LOVING Penny Jordan

ROMANCE OF A LIFETIME Carole Mortimer

THE MOST MARVELLOUS SUMMER Betty Neels

TATTERED LOVING Angela Wells

GYPSY IN THE NIGHT Sophie Weston

PINK CHAMPAGNE Anne Weale

NIGHTS OF DESIRE Natalie Fox

DARK GUARDIAN Rebecca King

YOURS AND MINE Debbie Macomber

FROM THE HIGHEST MOUNTAIN Jeanne Allan

A FAIR EXCHANGE Valerie Parv

AFTER THE ROSES Kay Gregory

SPRING SUNSHINE Sally Cook

DANGEROUS ENGAGEMENT Lynn Jacobs

ISLAND MASQUERADE Sally Wentworth

STARSIGN

THE TRAGANA FLAME Jessica Marchant

Available from Boots, Martins, John Menzies, W.H. Smith, Woolworths and other paperback stockists.

Also available from Mills and Boon Reader Service, P.O. Box 236, Thornton Road, Croydon, Surrey CR9 3RU.